To
Lavonne & Bob
I hope you enjoy
Colorado adventure
With my best wishes always

Arla
11/12/95

Shadows on the Slopes

Shadows on the Slopes

Arla R. Jensen

A Geneva Book

Carlton Press Corp. ❖ New York

This is a work of the imagination. Any resemblance to places, or people living or dead is purely coincidental.

Copyright © 1995 by Arla R. Jensen
ALL RIGHTS RESERVED
Manufactured in the United States of America
ISBN 0-8062-5073-9

To Buz
my dearest husband and whookeeper,
with deepest love and appreciation.
Thanks for being there,
for being you.

Shadows on the Slopes

1

The crisp winter day dawned with a hint of a promise of snow. The group of people, dressed in their colorful ski apparel, dropped their bulky equipment on the ground and began to board the chartered bus parked outside the grey stone building. The Smith & Wheeler Advertising sign glistened in the early morning dew. Tints of pale mauve and bronze began to streak across the morning sky, soon to become a golden hue overlapping the layers of sunrise clouds. One of the skiers, an attractive blonde, bent down to adjust the bottom of her ski pants. She straightened up and hurried to the rumbling vehicle. The line waiting behind her to board the bus shuffled forward as she climbed up the steps. She chose one of the comfortable dark blue plush seats, and sat down, unaware that this day would turn out to be one of the most terrifying and confusing days of her life!

"Everyone aboard?" shouted the bus driver, as he turned his head toward his passengers. He clutched a paper cup in his almost frozen hand.

"That's it," came a voice from the back of the bus.

"Okay, let's go." The driver drained the contents of his cup. He threw it in the general direction of the trash can. The doors closed, and the vehicle headed towards the Crystal Hill Ski area, about 70 miles away.

Annette Howard settled against the back of the seat and sighed. She frowned and pushed back a lock of her curly blonde hair from her forehead. She was twenty-seven, slender, tall, with deep-set green eyes that, she had been told, could melt the hardest heart. There had been several men in her life, but most had been only superficial romances. Only one had she really fallen for, been close to marriage even. And he had betrayed her. It had taken a long time for her to admit their relationship had been wrong. It was one of the worst times of her life.

The vehicle continued toward the ski area in the Colorado mountains. Sounds of chatter could be heard in the background. The road to Crystal Hill was full of winding turns and narrow, almost threadlike passages. Annette gazed out the window at the passing scenery.

She wondered if the lodge looked the same, and pictured in her mind the rugged building and huge stone fireplace. There had been comfortable rust-colored leather sofas, and large and inviting deep brown overstuffed chairs. Covering the highly polished wooden floor was a thick, beautifully patterned rug. She snuggled down against the soft padding of the seat. There had also been plenty of memories of ski trips to Crystal Hill. How alive she had felt, loving a man who loved skiing, and her. At least she had thought he loved her. The wounds would heal eventually. Now she was going skiing for the first time in two years. It had been that long since she had skied with Herb....

"Hi, Annette," a cheery voice interrupted her thoughts. She looked up. Before her was the smiling face of Sherry Adams from the Design department of Smith & Wheeler.

"Hi, Sherry," Annette replied. "Are you anxious to get out on the slopes?"

"Can hardly wait. I'm really looking forward to trying out my new skis," she said with a wide grin. "How about you?"

Annette paused. "Well it's been a while since I've been skiing. It'll probably take me a while to get used to them again. But it'll be nice to be outdoors and feel the wind rushing in my face."

"You and Herb used to go skiing a lot, didn't you?"

"Yes, we did," Annette said, glancing away, an unhappy look on her face.

Sherry looked carefully at Annette. She frowned briefly, and immediately changed the subject. "Would you like to room together at the lodge?"

"Sure, that would be great," Annette answered with enthusiasm. "It's been a while since we've had a chance to get together and talk."

"You're right," Sherry agreed.

Annette smiled. Sherry was a fun person. She was attractive and had a dynamic personality. They had been friends since Annette had started working at Smith & Wheeler about three years ago. They had discovered they had a lot in common, and had done many things together.

"We're coming into Crystal," a shout came from the back of the bus.

"I'll see you later," Sherry said, and turned to go back to her seat.

"Okay," Annette replied. She looked down with satisfaction at her new ski outfit. She folded her parka on her lap. I hope I can feel comfortable doing this, she whispered to herself. She stared out the window as the bus lumbered up the last hill. The driver eased the big machine expertly into the parking space. A big sign stood a few yards away *Welcome to Crystal Hill Ski Lodge*. Annette joined the throng of passengers, now beginning to noisily jam the aisle, eager to get out of the stuffy air.

As the bus passengers slowly filed into the lobby of the Chalet Crystal, Annette looked around her. The day was going to be perfect for skiing. The clouds had parted, showing a clear blue above, with wisps of white and grey along the tops of the hills.

The clerk smiled admiringly at her as she approached the desk. After explaining that she would be sharing a room with Sherry Adams, she signed the register, took the key, and went to find their room. As she started walking down the hall, she saw Hal Newcomb, the group's leader. He was the head of the Creative Department at the agency.

"Hi, Annette," he called to her.

"Hi, Hal," she answered.

He walked over and put an arm around her shoulders. "Don't forget about the dinner we're having tonight here at the Lodge. It'll start at 8:00 in the Main Dining Room. I'll have tickets for it later."

"Okay, Hal. I'll be there, and I'll let Sherry know too. We're going to be rooming together."

"Great," he smiled and squeezed her shoulder. "See you later. Have a good day on the slopes."

"Thanks, Hal. You too." Annette watched him walk away. She wondered how sometimes he could be so nice, and other times be so obnoxious and demanding. He had a big ego, and always tried to make the women at the agency think he was so macho. He was fairly good looking, but nothing terrific. Oh, well, she thought, dismissing him. It takes all kinds. She took a deep breath and headed down the hall to room 163.

Inside, she set her suitcase down on the nearest bed and surveyed the room with pleasure. It was rather small, but had been decorated by an expert hand. The furniture was all of a heavy dark oak. It consisted of the two beds with carved headboards, a tall dresser, and two wooden chairs. The bedspreads were of a heavy material with a white and blue design resembling a mountain scene. There were attractive white drapes at the window, drawn back with dark golden cords. The floors were highly polished. A royal blue throw rug lay between the beds, and another was on the far side of the room. But the main object that caught her eye was a magnificent painting. It looked like it had been transferred there straight from the Swiss Alps.

Annette stood transfixed for a moment. She caught her breath as she stared at the painting. The place looked so familiar. She recognized the area. Those snow-covered peaks. It was Switzerland. Near Lucerne. As she continued to gaze at the picture, Sherry entered the room. Annette smiled at her.

"Well, you finally made it through the madding crowd," she said, brightly.

"Yes. That lobby is a madhouse. There's a ski convention here, and another company has a group here, too. I can just imagine what the slopes will be like." She sat down on the other bed. Her gaze fell on the painting.

"What a beautiful scene," she exclaimed. "It looks like it might be Switzerland."

"It is," Annette replied, looking down at the floor. "It's Lucerne—where I went skiing with Herb a couple of years ago." Quick, hot tears came to her eyes.

Sherry looked at Annette intently. "I know that you've gone through a rough time, Annette. You seemed to be so much in love with him. Everyone at the agency thought you'd be getting married. Then, all of a sudden it was over. And I've never seen you so upset and depressed." She paused. "What happened? I know you didn't want to talk about it then, but I think it's about time you did. It's still bothering you."

Annette sighed and took a deep breath. "It's a long, complex story, Sherry, One of these days I'll tell you about it. Right now I just want to get on with my life and try to put it all behind me."

"Okay, if that's what you want. I'm going to go up to the top of the mountain with John and a group of the guys. Do you want to come with us?"

"No, thanks anyway," Annette replied, slowly. "I think I'll wait a bit and get my 'ski legs' again. It's been a while."

"Okay. I'll see you later, then."

"Oh, Sherry, Hal said there's a dinner tonight in the Main Dining Room at 8:00. If I'm going to be late, I'll leave you a message at the front desk."

"Okay. Have fun." Sherry went out, and the door clicked behind her.

Annette sat down on the edge of the bed. Again she looked up at the painting. Memories came flooding back. She and Herb had met here, at Crystal Hill, on a group ski trip. He was tall, with dark hair and sparkling brown eyes. His favorite color was blue. Blue. And he wore it well. He was her teacher. He was always there to ease her falls, to soothe her hurt pride, to tell her to bend her knees, to relax. And he was her lover. They talked seriously about marriage. Everything seemed wonderful. Until one evening when her whole world fell apart.

He seemed nervous. Restless. She asked him what was wrong. He began pacing across the room, but said it was nothing. She was persistent. "I don't know how to tell you this . . ." he began.

Annette felt her heart almost stop. "Tell me what?" she said with concern. She had no idea what he was about to say. But she was afraid.

He hesitated. "Annette, I don't want to hurt you . . . but . . ." He finally admitted that before he had met her, he had been involved with another woman. Her name was Helen. She had become his common-law wife. He had loved her, but they had separated. But now she wanted him back. She was pregnant with his child and would bring legal action against him if he refused. She could ruin his career. His life. She had threatened to do whatever she could to make life miserable for him. And she would. He didn't doubt that for a minute. Her father was a lawyer who had connections of all kinds.

Annette trembled at the thought of how incredulous that was at the time. He had lied to her. He said she was the only one, that he'd never been married to anyone, ever. Liar. Cheat. She remembered vividly the scene that night. The cold accusations. The tears. The deep hurt that would not go away. She tried to make some sense out of the whole situation. She wanted to awaken from the awful nightmare. The dreams of the future, shattered with this confession. She remembered, as if it were yesterday, how he had said he had tried everything, but there was no way around it. He had acted like a beaten puppy. There was nothing he could do but go back to Helen. Annette had been stunned.

"I can't believe this!" she screamed, as the tears streamed down her cheeks. "Is it really your child, Herb, or is she just saying that to get you to come back to her?"

There was a moment of hesitation. "No, it's my baby, Annette," Herb whispered, huskily. He lowered his head, and covered his face with his hands.

"You bastard," she shouted. "You lying, cheating bastard. What about me? What about us? What were you going to do, marry me and have her on the side?" She stopped to catch her breath and looked him directly in the eye. "What is it with you? Do you think this has all been a game with me? How could you do this to me? Why didn't you tell me the truth? I can't believe you were seeing her, too. We had talked about getting married. For god's sake, don't you think I care about you? Don't you think I love you?" she choked on her tears. It was all too much. It had to be a nightmare. But she couldn't seem to wake up.

"Oh, Annette, I love you more than you'll ever know," he said. "I didn't want to lose you. I was afraid I guess. I don't know. I never expected this to happen. I thought I could end things with Helen. I swear I didn't know she was pregnant. Oh God, Annette, I didn't mean to hurt you. You are the world to me. You're like a jewel. And I felt myself come alive in your presence. I really love you." He began to cry and tried to put his arms around her.

Annette pushed him away. Her head was reeling. She couldn't think.

"You damn liar," she shouted, getting up from the couch. With tears blinding her eyes she stumbled to the front door. "What a fool I've been to believe anything you ever told me. Get out, Herb! I never want to see you again." She opened the door. "You heard me, get out!"

He hesitated. "Annette, please . . ." He held out his hand, but she looked away. Then he left. She heard his footsteps on the stairs, as she turned her head and clung to the door for support. She had slammed the door shut. He was gone. . . .

Annette wrapped her arms around her body and rocked back and forth. It all seemed such a long time ago. She remembered, with pain, how she sat and wept that night. The shock. The empty, lost feeling that had swept over her then, had all but returned. She had loved a liar. A cheat. He had swept her off her feet. He had made her believe they would have a future together. The feeling of hatred, of betrayal, was so strong. But so were the feelings of love, and an overwhelming sense of loss.

Her thoughts were suddenly interrupted by a knock on the door. She got up quickly and opened it. There stood Joan, one of the women from the agency.

"Hey, Annette, aren't you going up on the slopes?"

"Why, yes," she replied, trying to wipe away the tear streaks. "What time is it?"

"About eleven. A bunch of us are going to grab a sandwich and then head on up the hill. Want to come along?"

"Sure, come on in for a minute." She went into the bathroom and glanced into the mirror. Noting the black mascara streaks under her eyes, she rubbed them with a tissue, ran a comb quickly through her hair and dabbed on some lipstick. "Okay, let's go," she said to Joan. They left the room and headed in the direction of the snack bar.

After lunch, Annette went back to her room to put on her parka and get her scarf and gloves. She had changed her mind about going up the lift with the others. She wanted to be by herself for a while. It was a strange feeling to be here at Crystal Hill again. And she had to get used to it. And to skiing again, as well.

She left the lodge and went over to the Ski Hut, where the group's ski equipment was kept. She planned to spend some time on the lower slopes before tackling the upper areas. She collected her skis and boots, and took them to a bench where she could sit down comfortably. There were several people there, apparently from the Ski Convention. They were busily putting on their boots and chatting amiably.

Annette straightened up for a moment. She glanced over at the other end of the room. Near the wall stood a tall, nice-looking, dark-haired man. He was wearing a blue ski sweater. Her breath caught in her throat. Her heart began racing. She couldn't believe it. He looked like Herb! She looked down. Her throat felt dry. No. I don't even want to talk to him, she thought, wondering how she could avoid it. He was the last person she wanted to see. She glanced back at him again. The man moved his head, and relief swept over her. It wasn't Herb after all. She took a deep breath. I'm really losing it, she thought. My imagination is just running rampant. As she finished lacing up her boots, the stranger began walking over towards her.

"Hi, are you here with the Ski Convention?" he inquired.

"No," Annette replied rather nervously. "I'm with our office group."

"Oh, which group is that?" he asked.

"Uh, Smith & Wheeler," Annette responded, getting to her feet. She began collecting her skis and poles. She wondered what he wanted.

"Oh, yeah, that's the advertising agency, isn't it?" He rested his foot on the bench. He appeared to be in his early thirties, and was quite attractive.

"Yes," she said adjusting her gloves. He made her nervous.

The man smiled, and extended his hand to her. "I'm Eric Woodward," he said with a pleasant grin.

"I ... I'm Annette Howard," she stammered, as she shook his hand. She looked up at his face. He could have been Herb's twin brother! The resemblance was uncanny and most unnerving. His hair was the same shade of dark brown. But his eyes were what caught her attention. They were deep brown and sparkling. And they had a sensitivity about them. Her heart began hammering. Perspiration began to trickle down her sides. She stood frozen, unable to think or speak.

"Are you going up to the top?" he inquired, with an admiring glance at her.

"I don't know. I hadn't really planned to. I haven't been skiing for a while," she murmured. She looked at him doubtfully. She felt confused.

"Oh, I see," he replied. He gave her a winning smile. "Well, Annette, it's really not that bad up there, just a few more hills. I'm sure you could handle it. The view is really nice up there. I'd like for you to go up with me. C'mon, give it a try."

Something in the back of Annette's mind was telling her not to go, not to listen to this man. But it was drowned out by the smile, the sparkling eyes, and his smooth, persuasive manner. She paused. "Well, okay," she said, a bit uneasily. There was something about him. She felt drawn to him. They put on their skis outside. He helped her adjust her bindings. Then they headed toward the lift. After waiting a few minutes, they boarded the chairlift. Annette watched the snowy ground drop away from underneath her. She was tongue-tied. What am I doing, she thought to herself. Here I am going to the top of the mountain with a man I don't know, who reminds me of Herb! I must be crazy! But he does seem nice. I guess it's no big deal. I can handle it, she decided. She had no idea how her decision to accompany him would change her life forever! Eric Woodward seemed to be at home on the ski lift. He was charming and an easy conversationalist. He talked about skiing. He had gone to some of the places she and Herb had. Great, she thought, just what I needed to hear!

"Do you come up here to Crystal Hill often?" she inquired.

"Well, I used to," he replied. "But I haven't been here for quite a while. "My brother and I used to come up a lot."

"Oh, do you both live in the area?" she asked.

"Not now," he replied. "He got married and moved to another town."

Annette glanced at the man sitting beside her. She felt a chill go through her. "Where do you live?" she asked.

"Englewood," he said casually. "And you?"

"Aurora," replied Annette. She was trying to shake off the uncomfortable feeling that had settled over her.

"Oh, yeah, I've been to a great Chinese restaurant there, The China Doll. Do you know where it is?"

Annette knew it well. She and Herb had frequented it. "Sure, I've been there several times," she said, wanting to change the subject. "What kind of work do you . . ."

But her voice was lost in the wind. Eric Woodward seemed not to hear. She looked around and surveyed the view. It was breathtaking. They were on top of the world.

Suddenly, there was a piercing, grating noise. The chairlift shuddered and came to a halt. Annette glanced at Eric. He shook his head.

"What's going on?" she asked anxiously.

Eric looked around. "I think the ski lift machinery has jammed." There was a note of concern in his voice.

Annette looked down. It was a long way to the ground. They had just passed the last cable platform. The top of the mountain was still a good distance above them. She was scared. Don't panic, she told herself. Everything is going to be okay. But the seat was swinging back and forth. Annette gulped a breath of air.

"Maybe they'll get it going again soon," she said bravely. But she felt that was optimistic. She was wishing she had never agreed to go skiing at the top of the mountain, with this man.

2

As the sun passed behind the mountain, there wouldn't be much daylight left. The air was getting chilly. They were suspended high above a band of evergreen trees, with a surrounding snowy terrain. Eric knew Annette was anxious. He wasn't too calm himself, but he tried not to let it show. He knew it would probably take a while for the maintenance crew to locate the problem. Then they would have to alert the ski patrol and rescue units to assist the stranded skiers.

"I'm sure they're working on the problem, and will have it fixed soon," he replied, trying to calm her. "Also, the ski patrol and the rescue people will be out to help the stranded skiers."

"But it's getting dark," she whispered, "and colder." She zipped her parka all the way up and wrapped her scarf more tightly around her neck.

Eric put his arm around her. He felt her shoulders shaking. "It's going to be okay. Don't worry, I have at least nine lives," he said, with a smile that belied his true feelings. He was more than a little concerned about their plight.

"Well, I hope you don't have to prove that you can land on your feet," Annette replied.

The sun reached the back of the mountain, and disappeared quickly, as if someone had pushed it. They were alone, two solitary figures hanging above the lengthening shadows of dusk which painted their way across the glistening snow.

A few minutes later, Eric felt a slight motion. The chairlift appeared to be inching forward on the cable. He wondered if it were his imagination. Then he was sure. It began moving slowly upward. He looked at Annette, smiled, and squeezed her hand.

"It's going to be okay," he said firmly. "We're going to make it to the top, after all."

Annette took a deep breath, and shut her eyes. "Thank God," she responded. She tried to quit shaking, but it was impossible to do so. At the top of the mountain the ski lift attendant grabbed the pole on their chair and slowed it.

"We were lucky on this one," he said. "One of the cables came loose. This part of the area has just been opened for night skiing."

Annette looked around and saw the colored spotlights shining on the snow. "It's beautiful," she shouted. There were beams of violet, gold and green shimmering on the snowy slopes. It looked like a color version of a winter wonderland.

Eric surveyed the landscape. "I didn't know they had night skiing up here." he said. "That's great!"

They sat down on some nearby rocks and adjusted their boots and skis. Annette asked Eric how long he'd been skiing.

"Oh, seven years or so," he replied.

"Are you here with the ski convention?"

"No, I came up with some people from Concord Engineering. We have a group that gets together for ski trips quite often."

Annette caught her breath. "Did you say Concord Engineering?"

"Yes, I work in their computer division."

A cold sweat enveloped Annette. "Do you happen to know Herb Edwards?" she asked warily. She didn't want to know the answer, but had to ask. She was not prepared, however, for Eric's reply.

"Sure," he laughed. "He's my brother. We both used to work at the East Denver facility. Why do you ask?"

"Your brother?" Annette's brain began whirling. This couldn't really be happening, she thought. She had to be in the middle of a horrible dream. Yes, that was it. She would wake up and everything would be normal again. But No. It wouldn't be. This was Herb's brother! Right here. With her! He didn't seem to recognize her name. Maybe he didn't know what the connection was with Herb and her . . . maybe . . . This was too much. . . . Here she was on top of a mountain with a man who had just sent her world into a crazy spinning-out-of control feeling. What next! What should she say?

"Oh, I know someone at the agency who knows him," she covered, as casually as possible. Her heart was racing. Her mind went totally blank. She felt a wave of dizziness.

Eric looked at her. "Are you all right? You look sort of pale, and strange."

"Sure, I'm fine," Annette answered, anxious to get away from him. She still couldn't believe it. Justified, or not, she felt some animosity towards this man. He was connected to a part of her life she had wanted to forget. And now she was face to face with it.

"Well, let's get out on those beautifully lit slopes," he said. He got up and headed towards one of the ski runs.

"You go ahead," said Annette. "I want to take my time. I need to practice a bit."

"No problem," said Eric. "Remember, I'm here if you need help. I'm not the greatest skier, but I do okay."

Annette watched him begin his run. He handled his skis expertly. He was completely at home on the slopes. She took a breath of the crisp evening air, and began to make her own way to the ski run. She wanted to forget everything, to ski as fast as she could and get away from him. But she knew that wasn't possible now. She would have to be patient, and careful. Of all the weird things to happen. Just my luck, she thought to herself. I'll play it cool, though. He'll never know who I am.

Eric skied down the hill. He watched as Annette completed her turn. "Isn't this great?" he exclaimed. "See, it's not such a difficult place. You're doing fine. You must have had a good ski instructor."

At the mention of that, Annette cringed. She went cold inside. If he only knew, she thought. I guess Herb didn't say anything to him about me. She smiled at the thought.

Eric noticed her smile, and completely misunderstood its meaning. "That's better," he said. "I was beginning to think you weren't enjoying my company. You seemed so solemn and uptight." He smiled at her. His eyes sparkled.

"Oh, no," Annette replied. "I'm having a great time. I was just upset by the problem on the ski lift coming up here." It wasn't entirely true, but it would suffice.

"Yeah, that wasn't much fun," Eric responded, "but the snow is great. So let's enjoy ourselves while we're here."

Annette agreed, and began to follow him down the next hill. Suddenly she remembered the group dinner. "Eric, do you know what time it is?" she called to him.

He skied over to her, came to a stop, and checked his watch. "It's about 7:30."

"Oh!" she said with dismay. "Our group is having a dinner at the lodge at 8:00. I guess we won't make it down in time."

"Oh, I'm sorry, Annette," Eric said. "I didn't realize how late it was. I'm afraid we'll miss it. We can have dinner together in the lodge later on, if you'd like."

Annette nodded, and said that would be fine. There really wasn't much they could do about it now. He did seem nice. In spite of the fact he was Herb's brother. But she was concerned about not appearing at the Smith & Wheeler dinner. She had asked Sherry to save her a place. Annette knew she would be would be worried about her if she didn't show up or leave a message.

At the lodge, Sherry went to the front desk to see if there was a message from Annette. It was almost 8:00 and no one had seen her since early afternoon. Sherry was concerned, even though she had said she might be late. There was no message. She picked up the tickets for both of them and went into the dining room. She saw Hal Newcomb talking with one of the waiters.

"Hal, have you seen Annette anywhere?" she inquired.

"No, not since this morning," he replied. "Why, isn't she here?"

"No, and there's no message from her at the desk. I haven't seen her since before lunch. I'm getting kind of worried."

Hal noted the look of concern on Sherry's face. "Oh, I'm sure she's all right," he said. "She'll show up. Maybe she met someone on the slopes and went for a drink somewhere."

Sherry doubted that. Annette would have at least left a message if she had gone off with someone. She had planned to attend the dinner. Sherry glanced at the clock on the wall. It was 8:15.

3

Annette and Eric skied down the brightly-lit snowy slopes together. It was exhilarating. Annette was actually enjoying herself. They began to encounter icy patches here and there, however, and one of them was particularly treacherous. The edges of Eric's skis caught the slippery snow, and he began to slide. He fought to get back in control. He cut to the left and back again to the right. But in doing so, he overran the actual ski run and headed towards an outer area of virgin snow lined with trees.

Annette saw what was happening. "Look out, Eric," she called, frantically.

Eric saw the tree branches flying by his head. He tried to manipulate his skis, but the snow was now almost pure ice. Despite his best efforts, he was unable to stay in control. His years of skiing experience were all but useless in this situation. Annette knew he was in trouble. He was in an area that was off-limits to skiers, and with good reason. The snow was untouched. There were only trees and icy hills! He was gaining momentum in the direction of a large grove of pine trees. He tried to turn away from it, but his skis slipped on the ice-covered snow. He became airborne. Sailing head over heels over the edge of an embankment. He finally came to a stop, landing in a snowbank in a wooded area at the bottom of a steep hill.

Annette stood frozen. She couldn't believe what she had just seen happen. She called out to Eric, but there was no response. Not sure what to do next, she tentatively went towards where she had last seen him on the hill. Her skis were also getting slippery. She slowly went down the hill, making wide turns. Her heart was in her mouth. He could be hurt badly. He could be dead. She called out his name again. Silence. She sat down in the snow, and took off her skis. She stood them upright in the snow in the crossed position—the sign for skiers in distress. She was fighting back tears. The hill was steep. She thought she could more easily reach the area where he was by hiking down it in her ski boots. The wind was blowing harder now, and it was starting to snow. Slowly she trudged down the hill, using her ski poles to steady herself on the slick surface. She wasn't really sure where he was. She was terrified!

The lights were few in this section. Only here and there was the reflection of one of the colored spotlights. Annette found the footing extremely slippery. It was hard to see among the trees. She glanced to her left and saw a sign. Even in the dim light, the large red letters leaped out at her. "DANGER! AVALANCHE AREA—DO NOT ENTER!"

At the sight of the sign, Annette felt shaky. She stopped and drew in a breath. With some effort, she continued. What if she couldn't find him? She climbed over the ridge and looked down. She didn't see him. She slid down a few more feet. What she saw unnerved her. Eric was lying near a big tree, at the bottom of the hill. She couldn't see his legs, they were covered with snow. But as far as she could tell, he wasn't moving. I've got to get down there and see if he's all right, she murmured to herself. She was shaking with fear and cold. Cautiously, she inched her way down the hill. Several times she almost lost her balance and fell. Her ski poles helped her, but they were pushing further into the snow, and it was getting more difficult to pull them out. The snow was much deeper now, and the wind had increased. Annette stopped to catch her breath and put her scarf over her nose and mouth to ease the biting wind. then, she set out again. After a few more harrowing moments, she was able to reach the area where Eric lay. It was in shadow, but there were some shafts of light. Enough to make out the inert form on the snow. "Eric," she called out, with desperation, "Can you hear me? Please answer me." There was no response. She struggled through the deep snow over to him. He was lying on his back, and at first she thought he was dead. Then she saw his arm move. She knelt, and brushed the snow away from his forehead and eyes.

There was a deep gash on his head. He looked up at her, and tried to smile.

"Guess I didn't make that turn very well," he whispered, huskily.

He tried to move. Annette saw him grimace. "You hit some ice, and just kept going," she said. "It looks like your legs are buried pretty deep."

"Yeah, they're kind of stuck," he said. He was trying not to show too much discomfort, even though the pain was almost unbearable. "Well, this is a fine mess. How are we going to get out of here?"

Annette managed a brave smile. It was her turn, now, to comfort him. "Don't worry," she said, "I'm sure the ski patrol is out looking for us."

"Oh, sure," Eric gasped. "But how will they know where we are. We're sort of off the beaten path!"

Yes, Annette thought to herself, and in an avalanche area. She hoped he didn't know that. He had been heading down another hill, and probably hadn't seen the sign. She unwound her bright blue wool scarf from around her neck and folded it. She lifted Eric's head very gently and placed it underneath. "Look," she told the injured man, "I'm going to go up to the top of the hill and try to get some help. They'll never find you down here unless someone lets them know where you are."

"I guess you're right," he said with some effort. "I'm sure sorry about this, Annette. It just happened so fast. Boy, if my ski instructor could see me now...."

"Who was your ski instructor?" Annette asked absently.

"My brother, Herb," he replied. "He'll never let me forget this."

His response brought Annette back to the present situation with a jolt. It only served to make her more nervous and shaken. Under the circumstances, she had almost forgotten who this man was, lying injured here in the snow. Almost. She wondered vaguely to herself, what were the odds of meeting Herb's brother? Here! It must be at least one in a million! She adjusted her headband and gloves.

"I'll be back as soon as I can," she said, arising to her feet, "hopefully with some assistance. We'll get you out of here and get some medical help, somehow." But she had no idea how she was going to do that. She didn't know if the ski patrol was around, or where to look for them. And she realized, with a sinking feeling, that not only his life was in jeopardy, but hers, as well. It made her more determined than ever to find help!

Eric managed a small wave. "Thanks for all you're doing for me.

I really appreciate it. You're quite a woman, Annette," he said in a loud whisper.

"Well, I'm sure you'd do the same thing for me," she said, trying to dismiss the compliment. She didn't want him to see how it affected her. She was close to tears. She grabbed her ski poles, and began crossing the snow to the bottom part of the hill. Then she began the long, arduous trek up. She was fervently hoping the ski patrol was looking for them. They wouldn't have any idea where Eric was, unless someone told them. She said a prayer as she ascended the first hill. At the top of it she paused to catch her breath. Then she continued up to the next plateau.

4

The ski patrol was out looking for lost skiers, especially those who had gotten caught on the chairlift. Most of them were accounted for, but the leader, Bill Carson, wanted to continue his search at the top of the mountain. He needed to see if anyone who required help was still up there. He had just received a report on his radio from the lodge, that a man and woman were still missing. It was believed they had been on the defective chairlift to the top of the mountain. The night skiing had been cancelled, but the lights were still on. He and his crew began their hunt for the skiers about three-quarters of the way up the mountain. They had spotlights, and medical kits, and a medi-vac helicopter was based nearby. Bill knew how treacherous the hills could be when they got icy. It was getting colder. Big, fluffy flakes of snow were falling again, making visibility difficult.

As the snow began falling, Annette found it increasingly hard to see. She dropped to her knees several times. She tried to catch her breath, and get a firmer footing on the snow. This was not easy. She was getting very tired, and her muscles were aching. She climbed the last few yards to the top of the second hill on her hands and knees, ski poles dragging behind her. She stood up, gasping for breath. She was surrounded by a world of white. A few minutes later, she thought she heard sounds. Voices? Maybe. Or was it the wind playing tricks on her? She wasn't sure. But it sounded like someone. She listened carefully. Again, she heard it. This time she knew for sure it was voices. Men's voices! But she didn't know where, or how far away they were.

She screamed. "Up here! I'm Up Here," and began waving her ski poles frantically. It was a futile effort. Whoever it was, they couldn't hear or see her. She kept on shouting. But against the wind, it was all but hopeless. Nobody knows that I'm here, she thought. Then she remembered she had left her skis standing crossed on this hill, somewhere nearby. She didn't know exactly where. She prayed that the ski patrol would find them and know there was a skier in trouble. She continued to shout into the cold night air. She was desperate. She had to get help soon.

Farther down the hill, Randy, one of the ski patrol members, saw a pair of crossed skis standing upright. He knew only too well what that meant. Someone was in trouble. He began searching for the owner. In the distance he heard a voice. Very faint. He called to the others, to let them know he had found the skis. He heard the voice again. It sounded like it was above where they were.

Annette began shouting again. Her voice was getting hoarse. "Up here, please come up here. We need help," she cried. She didn't know which direction to go.

Bill Carson directed his ski patrol team towards the sound of the voice. As they ascended the hill, on their snowmobiles, they saw a figure waving. They crossed the snow-packed ground over to where Annette stood.

Annette cried out again, "We need help." she saw the snowmobiles coming and ran towards the red-jacketed figures. Emotion overcame her, and she threw her arms around Bill. She wept into his shoulder. "Oh, thank God you're here," she sobbed. He held her for a moment, then gently drew her away. "It's okay," he said softly. "What are you doing up here so late?"

She managed to blurt out words between sobs. "We were . . . on the chairlift . . . it stopped . . . we were stuck for a while . . . then it started again and we . . . came up here to ski, but my friend . . . Eric . . . he fell . . . and . . ." She burst into tears.

"It's all right, now tell me exactly what happened," Bill said, kindly, trying to calm the nearly hysterical Annette.

Annette took a deep breath, and began to tell him how Eric had slid on the ice and gone out of control, and over the edge of the hill into the valley. She told him there was a sign denoting an avalanche area near where he was. The other members of the ski patrol listened to her tale, almost in disbelief.

"He's alive," she said, "but he's hurt. I came back up here to see if I could find someone to help us. I heard voices below me, but couldn't get your attention. I was praying that you'd find my crossed skis, and know someone needed help. There's no way that you'd be able to see us down where Eric is. It's dark, and way off the trail." She paused to catch her breath. "I don't know what I would have done without your help. I don't have a clue how to get down to the ski lodge."

Bill smiled. "Don't worry about it, we'll get you down. Okay, guys," he said to his team, "we'll have to see if we can get down there and get him out without calling for the helicopter." He radioed for more assistance. There was another patrol team on the lower slopes.

Annette watched as the ski patrol checked their equipment and prepared themselves to head down the hill to where Eric was. Bill Carson turned to one of his crew. "Randy, you stay here with her..." He turned to Annette. "I'm sorry, I don't know your name..."

"It's Annette Howard," she replied quickly.

"All right, Annette, I'm Bill Carson, and this is Randy Matthews," he said, introducing the tall man standing next to him. Bill radioed to the lodge that they had found one of the lost skiers, and were on their way to rescue the other one. He asked for them to have the helicopter ready to stand by, just in case. "Okay, let's go," he said to the group. He turned toward Annette. "You said he was in the valley of the avalanche hill, down by the trees?"

"That's right," she responded. "Do you want me to come with you and show you exactly where he is?"

"No, that's not necessary," said Bill. "You'd better stay here, we'll find him. I know that area, it's Crystal Valley." He looked at the members of his team. "That can be a dangerous area sometimes," he said solemnly. "You just look at that snow and it can start to slide. We'll have to be real careful." He caught the worried expression on Annette's face. "Don't worry. We'll get him out okay," he told her, "It'll just be a bit tricky, that's all."

As the ski patrol team headed towards the hills to rescue Eric, Randy tried to comfort Annette. "It's going to be okay," he said gently. "Those are outstanding guys. They'll find your friend, and take good care of him." He noticed the fresh tears begin sliding down her face.

She looked up at him. "I hope so," she said, quietly sobbing. It had been quite an ordeal for her. She was exhausted, and worried about Eric.

Bill Carson and his men made their way over the first hill. They came to the top of the second one. The avalanche sign stood forbiddingly at the edge. He was concerned that they might have to bring in a helicopter to rescue Eric. It depended on exactly where he was, and how badly he was hurt. Bill didn't want to think about the consequences if an avalanche began during the rescue. This was very possible, especially with the vibration from the helicopter. Leaving their snowmobiles at the top, the team continued over the ridge and down the other side of the hill into the valley. There, near a grove of trees, they saw a form lying in the snow. "There he is," Bill called out, "Over there by those pine trees."

Eric was barely conscious, when the team reached him. They removed the snow from his legs, and did a quick examination. It appeared that one leg was broken. He had numerous cuts and bruises on his arms, and a gash on his head. Bill quickly assessed the situation. Eric could also have internal injuries. He had taken quite a fall. The only way to get him out of here was going to be by helicopter. There was no other choice.

"Code One, this is Carson One," Bill spoke into his two-way radio. "We've got a seriously injured skier in Crystal Valley. Request helicopter assistance."

The response came back, "Carson One, this is Code One. What is exact location of injured skier?"

Bill told the pilot, Jeff Banks, where Eric was. He really was concerned about sending the helicopter into that area, but he had no choice. "We'll illuminate the area for you," Bill said. "There's a fairly large, flat area where you might be able to land. But if the snow is too deep, we'll have to hoist him up to you."

"Roger, Carson One, we're on our way E.T.A. is 15 minutes."

Bill looked at the faces of his ski patrol team. "Well, this is going to be a challenge, guys," he said soberly. "Just say a prayer that we can get him rescued and all of us out of here before there's any avalanche activity." He radioed the situation to the other patrol team who were then on their way to the top of the mountain, where Randy and Annette were waiting. That team would take them down to the lodge, while Bill and his group would rescue Eric. He called Randy and told him what the situation was with Eric's rescue.

"How is Eric?" Annette inquired.

"Well, according to Bill, he's got quite a few injuries, but he thinks he'll be all right. They just have to get him out of there and to a hospital as soon as possible." Randy didn't want to alarm Annette, but Bill had said that Eric didn't look too good. He was concerned about his condition, and the possibility of an avalanche, as well. A few minutes later, the other ski patrol team arrived to pick up Annette and Randy. They boarded the snowmobile and headed down the hill to the lodge.

The chopper flew to the top of Crystal Valley Mountain and began circling. It had stopped snowing. The pilot searched for the ski patrol team. He was glad they had spotlights. The one on the helicopter had gone out earlier, and he hadn't been able to replace it yet. After a few moments he saw them, waving their lights above the silvery snow. He began the descent into the valley. The wind was gusting. Bill watched as Jeff Banks brought the helicopter gradually down close to the ground. The snow began to blow wildly. It was impossible to see anything. He went back up a few feet, and radioed Bill.

"Looks like that isn't going to work," Jeff said, with concern in his voice. "I'll see if I can come in a little more to the right. Maybe it won't be quite so blustery over there."

Bill was very concerned about the disturbance of the snow, and possible avalanche danger. He wanted to get Eric on board the helicopter quickly, and get himself and his ski patrol team out of there, before anything happened.

"Okay, go ahead and try it," Bill responded. "This is really a dangerous area, Jeff, so we want to get him out of here as quickly as possible."

"Roger, Carson One, will try another attempt on the other side."

This time, again, the plane was buffeted heavily by the wind and was unable to land. Jeff was able to hover just above the ground, long enough for Bill and the team to hook a rescue basket to the winch. The medical team on the helicopter were then able to bring Eric up and into the plane. A few minutes later, the helicopter was fully airborne and heading toward the city.

"Let's get the hell out of here," Bill called, and he and his team began to leave the area. They made it up the hill to the ski run before it started snowing again. There, they climbed onto their snowmobiles and headed down the hill to their operations base.

A scant 10 seconds later, the avalanche began in all its fury. Hurling tons of snow and ice and huge boulders down the side of the mountain, it completely buried Crystal Valley, where the rescue had just occurred. Only the eyes and ears of the night watched and listened.

The weary ski patrol team, with Annette and Randy reached the bottom of the hill. They only had to wait a few minutes for Bill Carson and his crew to arrive. Bill went over to Annette. "Your friend, Eric, is in good hands," he said. "He's been taken to Valley Hospital. It was kind of tricky up there, but we were able to get him airlifted out without any major problems."

Annette smiled a tired smile. "I can't thank you enough for all your help," she said, addressing Bill and the others. "You really saved our lives."

"That's what we're here for," Bill said, returning her smile. "You've been through quite an ordeal tonight. If it hadn't been for you, we might not have found your friend. I'd say you probably saved his life. Are you okay?"

"I'm all right. Just cold and very tired. And I have a few aching muscles," she said, flexing her arms.

"Some rest and a hot bath will take care of that," Bill said. He and his team waved good-bye to Annette. She began walking slowly towards the lodge. Her feet felt like lead, and her head was aching unbearably. She pushed open the big glass doors. Several groups of people were standing around. Sherry saw her come through the door, and ran to meet her. She threw her arms around Annette and embraced her. Tears shone in her eyes.

"Oh Annette, my God I'm glad to see you," Sherry cried. "Are you all right?"

Sherry's concern unleashed a flood of emotion from her friend. Up to this point, except when the ski patrol had found her, she had been relatively calm and in control. But now she began trembling. She became aware of hot, salty tears cascading down her face. Unstoppable. "Sherry, it has been an unbelievable day and night," Annette sobbed into her shoulder.

Several of the co-workers from Smith & Wheeler, as well as people from Concord Engineering, gathered around Annette. They began asking questions about the rescue. They had heard about it from the lodge personnel. Annette was almost unable to talk. Utter exhaustion and emotion had drained her. She briefly told them the ski patrol had rescued both of them, and that Eric had been taken to the hospital by helicopter.

Hal Newcomb came forward and put his arm around Annette. "You certainly had us all worried, when you didn't show up for the dinner. We heard some news about you being rescued by the ski patrol. I'm glad you're okay, Annette."

Annette looked up at him and smiled a wan smile. "Thanks, Hal. I appreciate your concern. I certainly don't want to go through anything like that again, EVER!"

"Who were you with up there?" he inquired.

Annette took a deep breath. "A guy I met over in the Ski Hut. His name is Eric Woodward, and he works for Concord Engineering. They have a group here at the lodge also. I just hope he's all right. He had a terrible fall and was hurt pretty badly."

"I'm sure he'll be fine," Hal replied. "You'd better get some rest, Annette, you look exhausted."

"I am way past being exhausted, Hal," Annette said, slowly. She wished him goodnight, and acknowledged the rest of the group with a wave of her arm. "Goodnight, everyone," she said. She turned towards Sherry. "Let's go to the room, before I pass out." The group in the lobby dispersed, and Annette and Sherry headed down the hall to their room. It had been a long and anxious night. The clock on the lobby wall chimed. It was 2:00 a.m.

Sherry turned the key in the lock, and held the door open for her friend. Annette staggered over to the bed and fell face down upon it. She was too exhausted to move. Sherry went over to her, and tried to help her out of her ski parka. "I have a feeling that something really strange happened to you, today," she said quietly.

"That's putting it mildly," Annette muttered. She sat up. "It's the most incredible thing that's ever happened to me," she said, shaking her head. "You won't believe what I'm going to tell you. Sherry. I can hardly believe it myself. It seems like a horrible nightmare. And I want to wake up, but I can't. Because it's real!"

Sherry stared at Annette. "Why, what happened?"

Annette looked back at her. She began to peel off her damp, cold gloves. She had gotten her second wind.

"First of all, you have to know what happened between Herb and me a few years ago. Then I'll tell you about yesterday. They're related."

For the next several minutes Annette explained to Sherry what had happened in her relationship with Herb, about the child, and how he had gone back to Helen. Then she told her about the ordeal with Eric.

"It all started innocently enough," she said, as she turned her attention towards removing her ski boots. "I was over in the Ski

Hut, getting ready to go up the mountain, and there was this guy, who I thought looked like Herb. . . ."

She continued to tell about her harrowing experience of being on the chairlift with him, later finding out that he was actually Herb's brother, and then about his accident and the ski patrol rescue. She paused and glanced over at Sherry. She was staring blankly at Annette. Her mouth was open and she was sitting motionless, looking at Annette in total disbelief. The whole thing sounded like a plot for a soap opera.

"Are you kidding me?" That guy you met was Herb's BROTHER?"

"I'm dead serious," Annette replied. Tears began to fall from her eyes. "No wonder he reminded me of Herb when I first saw him. Only his last name is different, so that threw me off the track. I didn't have a clue they were brothers until later."

"Does he know that you know Herb?" Sherry asked.

"I don't think so. When he told me he worked at Concord Engineering, I asked him if he knew Herb. That's when he told me that he was his brother. I just passed it off that I knew someone at the agency who knew Herb worked there. He didn't give any indication that he knew about me, or my relationship with Herb. I was so nervous, Sherry. I almost got sick. Eric was so nice . . . very charming and confident. And he's a good skier. I was torn between telling him the truth, and just pretending I didn't know anything. It was hard. But when Eric got hurt, all I could think about was getting help for him, and somehow getting both of us to safety. It was really scary up there. If it hadn't been for the ski patrol, I don't know what we would've done. We'd probably still be up there." Annette shivered at the thought.

"Thank goodness they found you, and were able to rescue him," Sherry said quietly. "Was Eric hurt badly?"

Fresh tears began to creep down Annette's face. She nodded her head. Sherry got up and put her arms around Annette.

"It's okay," she said comfortingly. "You've been through one hell of a time. Why don't we both get some sleep? We can talk more about it tomorrow."

Annette put her head in her hands. "Okay, good idea," she said, wiping the tears away. All she wanted to do was fall asleep and forget everything. She was too tired to take a bath now. She just wanted to collapse.

"Oh, why did this have to happen?" she said, shaking her head.

"Of all the weird and impossible situations..." She began to cry again.

Sherry handed her a tissue, as she, herself, felt tears coming. "I don't know, Annette, but I think you handled it all really well. Eric sounds like a nice guy. It's just unfortunate that he happens to be Herb's brother. That makes things sort of, well, complicated."

"Yeah, isn't that just my luck," Annette snorted. She took off her saturated ski clothes and put on her nightgown. "He really did seem nice." She paused. "There was an attraction there, I think, for both of us. Gee, I don't know if I can handle this, or even want to try. What a mess. I wish it were all a bad dream." She laid her head back on the pillow. Exhaustion finally overcame her and she closed her eyes and slept soundly.

The sun was streaming through the windows when Sherry awoke. She glanced at her watch on the nightstand. Nine fifteen. Annette was still asleep. She got up, showered and dressed quickly. Then she went down to the dining room, where Sunday brunch was being served. She got a small tray on which she placed some croissants and preserves, two cups of coffee and a few napkins. She took them back to her room. As she set the tray down on the table, Annette woke up and smiled sleepily at her. "Hi, what've you got there?" she asked.

"Energy food," Sherry replied with a smile. "Help yourself."

"Thanks, it looks great."

"How do you feel?"

"Okay, just kinda tired. My legs sort of ache."

"No wonder," Sherry said, as she took a sip of coffee. "After what they've been through. I'm surprised your whole body doesn't hurt."

"Do you know what time we're supposed to leave today?" Annette inquired.

"I think probably around noon."

Annette took a bite of a croissant. "I'd like to find out where they took Eric, if I can. I think it was Valley Hospital, but I'm not sure."

"The guy at the front desk would probably know," Sherry answered. "Did you want to try and see him before we leave?"

Annette paused for a moment. "No, but I'd like to know how he is," she said.

Sherry glanced at her. "Well, it's after ten, so you'd better get up. We have to pack. We're supposed to meet in the lobby around noon."

"Oh gosh, I didn't know it was so late. I'd better get moving."

5

Annette slowly opened the door to the hospital room. She had a bunch of flowers in her hand. Eric Woodward lay quietly, his forehead swathed in bandages. His head was turned towards the wall. Annette hesitated, then moved toward the bed. She drew in her breath, and gently reached out to touch his hand.

"Eric," she called softly. The bandaged figure in the bed stirred slightly, and moved his head towards the voice.

"Hello Eric," she said again. Their eyes met. His were filled with pain. This was the man with whom she had shared a terrible ordeal several days ago. It seemed like years.

"Hi," he responded weakly, looking at the tall, slender blonde standing before him. He tried to smile. But it was difficult.

Annette moved closer to the bed and set the flowers on the chair. "How're you doing, ski partner?" she said in a gentle voice.

"Well I won't be on the slopes for a while," he said, glancing down at the cast on his leg. The smile faded.

Annette took his hand in hers. "I wasn't sure that I should come," she said, blinking back tears. She felt very emotional about what had happened, but wasn't really comfortable with the whole situation. It was hard to know what to say or do.

"I'm glad you did," Eric said tightening his grip on her fingers. "How did you know where I was?"

"I checked with Valley Hospital, where you had been taken the night of the accident. They said you had been brought here to Mile High."

He nodded. "Oh, I see," he said. "I heard that the ski patrol had a rough time trying to get me out of the valley that night. Did you know there was an avalanche right after they rescued me? I guess it completely wiped out Crystal Valley."

Annette stared wide-eyed at Eric. "What?" she said, trying to swallow over the lump in her throat that had unexpectedly appeared.

"Yeah, that's what I was told," he continued. "You know, if you hadn't been there to let the ski patrol know where I was, I probably wouldn't be around."

Annette suddenly felt shaky. She picked up the flowers and sank into the chair. Her hands were trembling. "I didn't know about the avalanche, Eric," she said quietly. "No one told me about that. I knew you were in an avalanche area, because of the sign at the top of the hill, but I didn't know one actually happened." She closed her eyes for a moment. She hadn't been prepared for this. She was the only one who had seen the accident, who had known where he was. It was actually true! Without her he wouldn't be alive. She opened her eyes.

"Well, pretty lady, I guess you're my heroine. You saved my life," Eric said, softly. He looked directly into her eyes. "I'm very grateful."

Annette found herself looking back at a pair of warm, sparkling brown, sensitive eyes. Herb's eyes, she thought, and glanced away.

"What's the matter?" Eric asked, with a note of concern. He noticed her discomfort.

"Nothing, really," Annette said, shaking her head. "It's just that I've never been considered a heroine before." It was true, but not the only reason. She couldn't tell him the real reason. And it wasn't because of his condition. "Anyone would have done what I did when they found a skier in trouble," she continued, trying to pass off the intensity of the moment.

Eric paused. "I'm really sorry we didn't have a chance to have dinner together that night, Annette," he said, sincerely. "Maybe we can after I get out of here. I'd like to get to know you better."

Annette stood up. She had mixed emotions about all of this. His words made her uncomfortable. She changed the subject. "Don't they have something to put these in?" she said, waving the bouquet.

"Maybe the nurse's assistant can get a vase or something. I think I'll go find her." She went towards the door. Eric's voice reached her. "Thanks for bringing the flowers, Annette."

She looked back at him. She was close to tears. "You're welcome, Eric. I'll be back soon," she said. She went out the door and leaned against the wall. She shut her eyes. Her head was spinning . . . What was she doing here? Why did she really come to see him? Her mind raced. She felt attracted to him, for whatever reason, but he was also Herb's brother. Could she trust him? Did she want a relationship with him? It was all so confusing. . . . Her thoughts were interrupted by a voice.

"Are you all right?" the nurse's assistant asked. "Can I get you something?"

Annette opened her eyes and saw a young, concerned face. "Oh no, I'm fine," she said quickly. "I need a vase for these flowers, though. They're for that room." She gestured towards Eric's door. The nurse's assistant smiled and took the flowers. "Thank you," Annette said. She took a deep breath and went back into his room. She looked at the bandaged face. He was half-asleep. A lump came into her throat, as she thought about what he had been through. "I'd better let you get some sleep," she said to him.

He nodded his head, slightly. "Okay," he whispered to her. "Will you come back again soon? Please," he added.

Annette looked at him. "Sure," she said with a bit of hesitation. "I'll see you later."

A couple of weeks later, Sherry and Annette were eating lunch in the cafeteria.

"Have you seen Eric lately?" Sherry asked.

Annette paused. "No, I haven't," she replied slowly. "In a way I wanted to go and see him again . . . but I don't know, I'm sort of afraid. I just can't shake the idea that he's Herb's brother. I know that probably sounds sort of strange. I keep saying that it doesn't make any difference. But I just can't convince myself."

Sherry took a sip of her iced tea. She set the glass down firmly on the table. Her gaze fixed on Annette's face.

"Look, Annette," she began, "you've got to forget about what happened with Herb. This is NOT Herb, okay? You went skiing with Eric because you wanted to. You didn't know anything about him then. Obviously there must have been some kind of attraction or you wouldn't have gone up to the top of the mountain with him, right?"

"Right," Annette answered sheepishly.

"And it sounds like he likes you, as well, even though things got off to kind of a rocky start with his accident."

Annette sat silently. She looked down at her plate, and toyed with a sprig of parsley.

"You can't judge him by Herb's actions, Annette," Sherry continued. "It isn't fair. At least give him a chance. Good grief, if you didn't know about the brother thing, you'd probably be thinking about some kind of relationship with him. From what you've told me, he sounds like a pretty nice guy."

Annette looked up. Tears were forming in her eyes. "I guess you're right, Sherry. I guess I haven't really been fair to him."

"Or to yourself, either," Sherry said. "You don't have to tell him anything about knowing Herb, or your relationship with him, unless you want to."

"No, no, I don't think I want to do that," Annette said, with a wavering smile. "That would really complicate things. Besides, he doesn't need to know about that."

Sherry finished her tea, and glanced at Annette. "Why don't you go and see him, and just let whatever happens, happen."

Annette listened and nodded. Okay, she thought, I can do this. She swallowed the last of her iced tea, and stood up. "Yeah, I think I will, Sherry. What's the worst that could happen, anyway?"

Sherry grinned and said, "Oh, maybe wedding bells, and who knows, maybe I'll be a bridesmaid one of these days."

Annette glared at her. "Hey wait a minute, don't rush things," she said laughing, as they walked to the exit doors.

Dark, ominous clouds were gathering as Annette drove into the parking lot. The sky looked like a blanket of charcoal. The wind was increasing, and rain was starting to fall. Big drops were hitting the windshield. She grabbed her umbrella and ran from the car to the main entrance of Mile High hospital. The rain began coming down hard as she reached the lobby door. When she reached the elevators at the other end of the hall, she pushed the button for the fifth floor and took a deep breath. Okay, she thought, she could do this. It wouldn't be the easiest thing in the world, but she needed to forget the thought that had nagged her for the past few weeks. Sherry referred to it as "the brother thing." Slowly, she opened the door to Eric's room. She hadn't seen him for a while, and didn't know what his condition was now.

Eric was sitting up in bed, reading. He glanced over at the door as it was opening, and smiled broadly at her. "Hi, stranger," he said brightly. "I was beginning to wonder if you were going to come and see me. It's been quite a while. It's good to see you."

Annette smiled back at him. "I've just been real busy at the agency, and working a bit of overtime," she said, feeling somewhat guilty. She tossed her jacket on the table, and put the damp umbrella by the wall. She pulled the chair over by his bed and sat down. It felt good just to see him. Her heart gave a small leap. "How're you doing?" she inquired.

"Real good," he answered. "It looks like I'll be out of here in a few days. Then the fun will start, having to use crutches, going to physical therapy, and all that. The doctor said I could go back to work soon, but we'll have to see how it goes."

She looked carefully at him. The bandage was gone from his head, and the bruises were healing nicely. One of his legs was still in a cast, and his right arm was bandaged, but for the most part he appeared to be in pretty good condition.

He grinned at her, his brown eyes twinkling, and reached for her hand. "I'm getting tired of this place," he said with a chuckle. "The nurses are pretty, but the rest is a drag." He squeezed her hand.

Annette laughed. "I'm sure they'll be sorry to see you go," she said, smiling at him. "You've probably been such a model patient . . ." She was interrupted by the door opening behind her.

"Hi there, bro," Eric shouted. "Come on in, I want you to meet the wonderful woman who saved my life on the mountain." He paused. "Oh, is Helen with you?" he asked.

Annette froze. She let go of Eric's hand, as if she had been burned. It couldn't be. This wasn't really happening, she thought. She heard Herb's voice answering. "Well, I certainly want to meet this mysterious lady." She didn't want to turn around. She couldn't. She sat there, afraid, motionless.

"Herb, I'd like you to meet Annette Howard," Eric said. His voice sounded like it was in a tunnel. Somehow Annette rose. It took all of her strength to stand up. Her feet were like lead. Her body unmovable. She turned and faced the man who was standing before her, the man she had loved. And hated. The man who betrayed her. She felt suffocated. The perspiration was running down her sides. She heard Herb catch his breath. She stared at him. His brown eyes looked deeply into hers, with a puzzled expression. She fought for control.

"Well, well, hello, Annette," Herb said, in that husky voice that had always turned her heart and mind to jelly. "It's nice to see you again. It's been a long time." He paused. His eyes swept over her. She felt the color rising in her face. "So, you are the one. Who would have ever believed it," he said sarcastically.

"It's nice to see you too, Herb," she mumbled with dry lips. She felt like she was going to faint. She wished the ground would open up and swallow her, that some unseen force would come and snatch her away from this incredible situation. But nothing came. Nothing happened. Eric didn't know anything. He didn't understand. She was alone in this, and was very uncomfortable.

"Hey, what's going on?" Eric said, staring first at Herb, and then at Annette. "Do you two know each other?"

Herb nodded, uncomfortably. His gaze was fixed upon Annette's blushing face. "Yeah, you might say that," he said. Annette was stunned. It was too much for her. She had to get out of there. Her head was spinning. The room was getting hotter. She felt like the walls were closing in upon her. She wondered, dimly, when the door was going to open again and Helen would appear. She didn't want to be here to meet her. She didn't want to be here at all! Her heart was racing. She moved towards the table, where she had laid her jacket. The whole room was a blur to her. "I can't do this," she shouted suddenly. She bolted for the door, grabbing her jacket as she fled. She needed air, quickly. This was a nightmare. She wanted to wake up. She had to. As she reached the door she heard Eric's voice calling her. "Hey, wait a minute, Annette."

She was shaking all over as she reached the hallway. Blindly, she headed for the stairs, avoiding the elevator. She felt dizzy. He had been as stunned by the meeting as she was, she thought. After going down a couple flights of stairs, she felt some cool air. She sat down and caught her breath. Soon she began to feel better. This was the very thing she had dreaded would happen. She couldn't handle it. When push came to shove, she had run away. But it was just too much. She didn't want to have to explain anything to Herb or Eric. It had been such a shock to see him, after all this time. And how sarcastic he had been. To think once she had been in love with him. But no more. If there had been any doubt in her mind before, now she knew for sure. She was a fool to think she and Eric could ever be friends.

When Annette reached the downstairs exit to the parking lot, she realized that she had left her umbrella upstairs in Eric's room. Never mind, she thought grimly, I'm not going back up there to get it. She zipped up her jacket and went out the door. The rain was still coming down, and the wind was blowing hard as she ran to the car. She climbed inside, wet and trembling, and laid her forehead on the steering wheel. She shut her eyes for a moment, started the engine and somehow drove to her apartment. She didn't even remember the drive home. She went in and collapsed on the sofa, letting the flood of tears begin.

Annette awoke to a ringing noise. She sat up, groggy, her eyes trying to penetrate the darkness. She couldn't tell if it was day or night. Her head throbbed as she moved in the direction of the ringing. She groped for the light on the table and turned it on. The noise stopped. She fell back on the couch and rubbed her forehead. She thought about her ordeal at the hospital, and wondered what to do. She couldn't go back there. Hopefully, she thought, Eric will leave the hospital in a few days and forget all about this. I'll never see him again, and I won't have to worry about him or Herb anymore. But deep inside she knew that probably wouldn't happen. She was sure Herb would tell Eric everything, if he hadn't already. The truth would come out about how they had met skiing at Crystal Hill, and all about their relationship, and Helen and the child and . . . Her thoughts were interrupted by the same noise again—the ringing of the telephone. She stared at the instrument, not wanting to answer it. She didn't feel like talking to anyone. She sat, unmoving, and the ringing stopped. She glanced at the clock. It was 11:30 p.m. She had slept for four hours. No wonder she felt groggy. She staggered into the bedroom and got ready for bed. She tried to go to sleep, but it eluded her. Shortly before dawn she dozed, only to be awakened soon thereafter by the shrill of the alarm clock.

Later that morning, Annette was sitting at her desk. She noticed someone standing in the doorway and looked up. Sherry was there with a worried expression on her face.

"Hi," Annette said, without enthusiasm.

Sherry looked at her. "You really look exhausted," she said, noting Annette's pale complexion and shadowed eyes.

Annette nodded. "Yeah, it was kind of a rough night. In fact, yesterday was pretty rough, too."

Sherry moved closer to Annette's desk. "I tried to call you last night," she said with concern in her voice, "a couple of times. I was worried about you."

Annette shook her head. "I was there, Sherry. I just didn't want to answer the phone," she said, unsmiling.

"What do you mean?"

"Something happened yesterday when I went to see Eric," Annette said. "It was awful."

Sherry sat down and rested her arm on the edge of Annette's desk. "Okay," she said, almost holding her breath, afraid of what she was about to hear.

Annette related the events that had occurred at the hospital the previous day. When she had finished, she sat back in her chair, her hands covering her face. "What do I do now, Coach?" she asked.

Sherry sat completely still, wide-eyed. "Oh my God," she said finally. "Annette, that is incredible. How awful."

"Yeah, it was kind of stressful," Annette said with a mock laugh. "I was afraid that something like that would happen, I guess, but I was praying it wouldn't. I just had to get out of there. You can call me chicken, or bimbo, or whatever you want, but I just couldn't take any more. Seeing Herb, and hearing his sarcasm. And knowing that Helen might be coming into the room any moment.... Poor Eric, he didn't have a clue what was going on."

"Well, he probably knows by now," Sherry offered. "I'm sure Herb filled him in on all the gory details. No, I don't think you're chicken or anything else, Annette. It's really a confusing and emotional situation. Anyone would be stressed out by it. I'd probably be a basket case, if it had been me."

Annette looked down. "I was really going to try and be friends with Eric, and, like you said, just see what happens. But now, with all of this other stuff going on, I think I'd better forget about him. He probably thinks I'm a bimbo, anyway."

"Oh, I don't think so," Sherry said with a smile. "But he probably thinks his brother is a jerk for what he's done to you."

"Yeah, sure," Annette said with a quick toss of her head. "Isn't this the kind of stuff movies and soap operas are made of?"

Sherry laughed. "Yeah, sort of," she said. "It would be funny, if this were actually a movie or soap."

"Yes, it would," said Annette quietly, getting up from her desk. "I wish it were all a bad dream that I could just wake up from, but unfortunately it isn't." She closed her eyes and leaned against the wall.

Sherry glanced at her watch. "It's almost lunchtime. Want to grab a bite?"

"I'm not really very hungry," Annette replied, "but I'll come and have some coffee with you."

"Okay," Sherry said, as she put her arm around Annette's shoulder. "Don't worry. Everything is going to be all right. Besides, a hundred years from now, it won't make a bit of difference."

"Yeah, I guess you're right," Annette said, as they began walking down the hall.

6

Weeks passed. The warm days of spring brought blossoming cherry trees, turning the landscape around Smith & Wheeler into a pink wonderland. Slowly, Annette's topsy-turvy world began to right itself. She had made no effort to see Eric again. She tried to put that traumatic chapter of her life behind her. So far she was succeeding. She was dating again, mostly double dates with Sherry and her friend Steve. They had introduced her to a nice guy named Bob, and the four of them were having fun going places together.

One warm and breezy summer day, Annette and Sherry were having lunch at an umbrella-covered table in the picnic area outside the office. They were engaged in conversation, when something caught Sherry's attention. She looked up and saw a man standing nearby on the walkway.

"What's the matter?" Annette questioned, noticing the puzzled look on Sherry's face.

"I'm not sure," Sherry replied. "There's a guy over there I've never seen before, and he keeps staring at us."

"Oh it's probably a salesman on his lunch hour or something," Annette replied.

"But this area is for employees only. All visitors have to check in at the lobby, don't they?"

"Yes, that's right," Annette responded. She turned away from the table to look at the stranger. No, she thought. It couldn't be. She felt her heart drop. She stared at the tall, well-built man who stood a few yards away. There was no doubt. It was Eric!

Sherry stood up to confront the intruder, but Annette stayed her with her hand. "Sherry," she began in a shaky voice, "that's Eric. Don't leave, please."

"Oh, my gosh," Sherry uttered in a low voice. "Are you sure?"

"Yes, I'm positive."

"What on earth is he doing here?" she questioned. "How did he know where to find you?"

"He knew I worked at Smith & Wheeler, remember?"

"That's right," she said, taking a deep breath. "The ski trip."

Annette nodded, turning back to the table. "I can't believe this, Sherry. Tell me it's my imagination. Please."

"I wish I could," Sherry said wistfully, again glancing at the man. "Brace yourself, he's coming this way. Maybe I'd better go."

"No, please don't leave me," Annette cried. "I can't go through this alone."

The tall, handsome figure slowly walked over to the table where the two women sat. He was holding a plastic bag. He paused, looking at Annette. She glanced at him. She felt her stomach flutter. She was not ready for this.

"Hello, Annette," he said, softly, looking down at her. He removed his sunglasses and set them down on the table, along with the bag. There were those incredible brown eyes!

"Hello, Eric," Annette answered, trying to sound friendly. Her palms were wet. She put her trembling hands on her knees, underneath the table. She felt like her mouth was made of clay. "I-I'd like you to meet my friend, Sherry Adams," Annette stammered, looking at him.

Eric extended his right hand to Sherry and gave her a beaming smile. "Nice to meet you, Sherry," he said, with sincerity.

"I'm glad to meet you too, Eric," Sherry responded, as she shook his hand.

There was an awkward pause. "Well, I've got to be going inside, I've got a lot of work to do," Sherry said briskly. She gathered up the paper lunch plates and cups and tossed them into the nearby trash can. She glanced at Annette, who sat unmoving. "I'll see you later, Annette, and it was nice to meet you, Eric," she finished. She got up from the table and walked toward the building.

Annette watched her go. She couldn't just get up and leave. She had to face him. She was tongue-tied. Finally, Eric broke the silence. "Is it all right if I sit down?" he inquired.

"Oh, sure," Annette gestured toward the seat on the opposite side of the table. "Please do." She looked hard at the man across from her. His eyes reminded her of deep brown velvet. She studied his face. He seemed unsure. She glanced down at the table and began toying with her sunglasses, not sure what to say or do. "You really caught me off guard," she said, finally.

"I wasn't sure if I should come here or not," he said shifting his position in the chair. "I didn't know how to get in touch with you. I didn't know where you lived, and I found out you had an unlisted phone number. Then I remembered when we were at Crystal Hill, you said you worked for Smith & Wheeler. The lady in the lobby said you were out here, and it was okay for me to come into this area to see you. I hope you don't mind." He took a deep breath.

Annette listened. "No, that's fine," she said, wondering why he had bothered to come.

"Besides," he continued, "I have a couple of things that belong to you."

Annette gave him a puzzled look. "You do?" she asked doubtfully.

Eric chuckled. "Yes, Miss Doubting Thomas, I do. You may be wondering where your umbrella disappeared to. Well, you left it at the hospital on one of your visits, when you left in rather a hurry," he said briskly. Annette cringed. He set it on the table. She waited. "And the other thing is this."

He began taking something out of the plastic bag. Annette felt her heart stand still. She could see the deep blue color of the item. It was her wool scarf. The one she had placed underneath his head, as he lay injured in the snow. Her fingers brushed his as he handed it to her. She felt a current run through her whole body. She caught her breath as she looked at the scarf, and felt its softness. Tears came to her eyes.

"That was quite a time, wasn't it," she said quietly, remembering the night of the accident. In some ways it seemed a long time ago. But in other ways, it was like it had happened yesterday.

"Yes," he said solemnly, "It was quite a time."

"Thanks, Eric," she said, gently. "I had no idea what had happened to it. I just figured it had gotten lost that night, somewhere on the ski slopes."

He looked at her face more closely. "No, it went with me to Valley

Hospital, and then I took it with me to Mile High Hospital. I was pretty sure it belonged to you." She sat back in her chair and focused on his face. The breeze was ruffling his hair. Where the sunlight caught it, it sparkled a deep-bronze. She looked down at the table. She couldn't believe this was actually happening, that he was here, sitting across from her. But she still wasn't sure why he was here. Was it just to return her things, or did he really want to see her? Did he know about she and Herb? All these questions were swimming around in her head, as she struggled to maintain some equilibrium.

"How are things going for you?" he asked, interrupting her swirling thoughts. "Oh, fine," she replied easily. "And for you?"

"Pretty good," he replied. "All the injuries have healed, and I'm back to work. I had quite a time with the crutches and I still have to go to physical therapy now and then, but the worst is over. Thank goodness!"

Annette smiled briefly. "I guess that's not much fun, from what I've heard. I'm glad you're doing well, Eric. You're looking good."

"Thanks."

They both sat silent for a few moments. Annette was thinking, "Okay, so you probably think I'm a bimbo for rushing out the door that day at the hospital, but I couldn't handle it when your brother came into your room, and I had to get out of there. . . ." She cleared her throat and said, "I guess I owe you an explanation for leaving in such a hurry when I was visiting you at the hospital that day." She looked away from him.

Eric shifted in his chair. She looked back at him. He was regarding her with a serious expression. He leaned towards her. "I think I understand now why you reacted that way," he said gently. "At the time I was confused, and hurt. I wish I had known that you had known Herb before. I had a long talk with him, and it made things a lot clearer. I love my brother, Annette, but sometimes he is such a jerk. He means well, but a lot of times he doesn't realize how he's hurting someone else. I'm sorry he hurt you. It must have been very hard for you to find out about Helen and the baby. He should have told you the truth." He paused. He wanted to touch her hand. Caress her fingers. But, he wasn't sure of her yet.

At the mention of the word "jerk," Annette stifled a smile. Well, Sherry was right, she thought. She looked away. She felt emotions pouring over her. She didn't want to let go. Not here. Not now. She fought for control. "I was so shocked when I found out you were his brother," she said hesitantly. "It was so hard to believe. I was kind of afraid to say anything to you about knowing him. But I probably should have. And I didn't know whether you knew anything about our relationship or not, so it was easier to pretend that I didn't know him." Annette shook her head. "Of all people to meet, with hundreds of skiers up there at Crystal Hill and all . . ."

"It must have been fate," Eric interrupted.

Annette smiled briefly "Or something," she added. "You know," she said looking at him, "for some reason I feel as if I've known you for a long time."

"I feel that way too," he replied. "Annette, would it have made a difference if you hadn't known we were brothers?"

Annette hesitated. "I don't know. I tried not to think about it, but it kept coming to mind," she said. She was beginning to feel uncomfortable. She had tried to put this all behind her. And here it was, all over again. The confusing feelings were beginning to surface. She wasn't sure she was ready for them. She felt like a trapped bird, struggling for freedom.

Eric leaned forward. He gazed into her eyes. "I have to know something, Annette," he said, looking serious. "Are you still in love with Herb?" Eric was almost afraid to hear her answer. Herb seemed to think she was. But he had to find out for sure.

His question caught Annette totally off guard. She hadn't expected this. She met his eyes. "No, Eric, I'm not. What happened between Herb and I was a long time ago. I guess I was very startled by his appearance at the hospital. That was the first I had seen or spoken to him since we broke up. I guess I felt anger and betrayal surfacing, and I handled it pretty badly. I'm sorry."

Eric relaxed visibly. "It's okay," he said. "I knew you were terribly upset then, but I didn't know why at the time."

"It was so ironic to meet you at the same place where we had met," she said. "In fact, when I first saw you in the Ski Hut, I thought you were Herb!"

Eric smiled. "That must have given you quite a start."

"It did," she confessed. "You look a lot like him," she continued. "You have the same kind of eyes, and some of your mannerisms are similar. It's uncanny. But your last names are different, so I didn't think there was any connection."

"Then you realized why there was such a resemblance after I told you we are brothers," he said.

Annette nodded her head slowly. "I really enjoyed skiing and talking with you, Eric. You really helped me to feel less scared when the ski lift jammed. Then the accident happened. I was so concerned about you. I knew I was the one that had to go for help. There was no one else around. But I was terrified," she confessed.

Eric watched her carefully as she spoke. "It really was a nightmare," he said finally. "All I remember was hitting some ice, and sailing through the air. And that horrible feeling of having no control of my skis. Also I recall landing in the snow, and not being able to move. But I guess I was pretty lucky all the way around. If you hadn't been there to get the ski patrol Annette, I don't know what would have happened."

Annette swallowed hard. She glanced at her watch. "Oh Eric, I've got to go in," she said quickly. "Even though my boss is on vacation this week, I've got some things that have to be done."

"Okay, I've got to be going too," Eric said, rising from the chair. "But first . . . As I recall, Annette, I owe you dinner. Remember, the night of the accident we were going to have dinner at the lodge? Only we never made it."

"Oh, I had forgotten about that," she said quietly.

"I haven't. Are you busy Saturday night?" he inquired.

She paused for a moment. "No," she replied. Her heartbeat was increasing.

"Do you like Italian food? I know a great restaurant with lots of atmosphere, excellent food, and outstanding wine."

"I love Italian food. It sounds wonderful," Annette said, smiling.

"Great," Eric said, grinning at her.

"What time?"

"How about 7:00?" He paused. "But I don't know where you live?"

"Oh, that's right," Annette said, laughing. She took out a notepad from her purse, scribbled down her address and phone number and gave it to Eric. "I'm glad you came here today," she said, looking up at him.

"So am I," he said. He picked up his sunglasses. "I'll be looking forward to seeing you on Saturday,"

The restaurant was crowded and bustling. Black-jacketed waiters scurried to deliver their food-laden trays to the red-covered tables. Candles cast a warm, rosy glow. The sounds of string instruments could be heard distantly. Antonio, the Maitre d' showed Eric and Annette to their private table in the far corner of the restaurant.

"Mr. Woodward, it is so nice to see you again," he greeted Eric, as he seated them. "Who is this lovely lady?" he inquired.

"This is Annette Howard," Eric responded with a smile. "She's a very special lady in my life."

The Maitre d' winked at Eric and smiled his best welcome smile at Annette. "I'm so happy to meet you," he said. "I hope you both enjoy your evening. Let me know if I can do anything for you." He bowed his head, slightly, as they thanked him, and returned to his post at the front of the restaurant.

Annette reached for the crisply folded red napkin that stood on the table before her, and placed it in her lap. She glanced briefly around the dining room. "This is a very nice place," she said, smiling at Eric.

"I thought you would like it," he answered, looking at her admiringly. She looked great, he thought, in her slightly low-cut black dress. The candlelight made her skin look creamy and soft. "I haven't been here for quite a while," he said, "but the food was great the last time I was here." He picked up the menu from the table and began to look at the choices.

A waiter appeared, clad in the black jacket and pants, with a spirited-looking red bow tie. "Good evening, my name is Mario, and I'll be your waiter for the evening. Would you like a wine list, sir?" he inquired of Eric.

Eric glanced at Annette. "Would you like some wine?"

"Yes, that would be great," she replied. The waiter handed Eric the wine list.

"And how about a cocktail before dinner?"

"Sounds good to me," Eric responded. "I'd like a bourbon and soda. How about you, Annette?"

"Vodka tonic, please," she replied.

The waiter wrote on his pad, and left the table. Eric picked up the wine list and began scanning the pages. "Let's figure out what we want to eat," he said, "then I'll pick a wine that's suitable."

"I'd like the fettucine Alfredo," Annette said.

"I'm going to try the veal scaloppine," Eric said. "I've had that here before and it was really good."

Mario returned with their cocktails and took their orders. Eric requested a light wine, and the waiter disappeared into the sea of black jackets at the other end of the room.

Eric looked across the table at Annette. "Well, it's a few months late, but we're finally having dinner together," he said. He lifted his glass, and Annette raised hers. "Let's have a toast," he said brightly. "To you, and Crystal Hill. If it weren't for you, we wouldn't be here tonight."

At the mention of those words, Annette began to tremble slightly. She touched Eric's glass with hers briefly and took a swallow. The vodka was cool and comforting. She glanced around her. Paintings of Italian landscapes flanked the walls. A marble fountain stood in the center of the room. The decor was subdued elegance. Lighting was low, and the glow from the candles lent a warmth to the room. The waiters moved with efficiency across the rose-colored plush carpeting. The friendly hum of conversation could be heard faintly.

Eric was watching his dinner partner with interest. "This is quite a place, isn't it?" he said, taking a sip of wine.

"It really is," she responded. "I love that fountain over there. It reminds me of one I saw in Italy a few years ago."

"That's one place I've never been," said Eric. "Someday I'd like to go there, and to Switzerland, too."

"Switzerland is a beautiful country," Annette replied. "My favorite place is Lucerne. It's so peaceful, right on the lake. There's a lovely covered bridge that's about five hundred years old, I think. It has paintings on the walls inside."

"Sounds beautiful," he said. "When were you there?"

Annette took a swallow of her drink. She had been there on her own years ago, but with Herb the last time. "Oh a few years ago," she said lightly. She passed it off, and changed the subject. "Do you enjoy traveling, Eric?"

"Yes," he said, smiling. "I've seen quite a lot of the U.S., and have been a few places in Europe: London, Paris, and parts of Germany. Some of it was on business trips, but I like sightseeing, too."

Mario appeared at their table with breadsticks and butter, and inquired if they wanted another drink.

They accepted and Eric said, "Speaking of traveling, "I think Herb and I will be going on a business trip to New York in a couple of months. Then, depending on how things go there, maybe over to London. There's a firm that is interested in one of our projects."

Annette glanced sharply at him. "Both of you?" she inquired. "I didn't think you worked together at Concord."

"Actually we don't," he replied, "but Herb has been working on a special computer program, and it just happened to work well with mine. The company in New York had some unusual requirements and my boss felt our project would be helpful. So we're going to go there and see what can be done."

Annette took a sip of her second drink. "How long will you be gone?"

"About a week or so," he replied.

Annette felt an unexplained chill come over her. The waiter arrived with their dinners, and conversation came to a temporary halt.

As Mario set their plates in front of them, Annette glanced at Eric and smiled. "Looks wonderful," she said with enthusiasm. He smiled and nodded in agreement.

Dinner progressed. They talked about many different subjects. The food was hot and flavorful, and the wine was an excellent accompaniment. Both Eric and Annette were caught up in the moment of enjoying the meal and each other's company. Neither spoke for a few minutes. Then Eric broke the silence.

"I'm so glad that you accepted my invitation to dinner tonight, Annette. I wasn't sure that you would."

Annette looked across the table at her dinner partner. "I'm glad I did too, Eric. I'm having a wonderful time. Thanks for asking me," she said, smiling. She felt comfortable. Happy. Content.

They finished the meal, and Eric poured the last of the wine into their glasses. "I really enjoyed this," he said to Annette.

"That was a wonderful dinner," Annette responded. "I've enjoyed it, too."

Mario appeared and inquired if they wanted after dinner drinks. Annette ordered an Amaretto on the rocks. Eric grinned. "Make it two," he said. "They have a dance floor in the other room. Do you like to dance?" he asked.

"I love to dance," Annette answered quickly. "At one time I wanted to be a professional dancer. But that idea came to a screeching halt after I was in an auto accident. My legs were badly injured."

Eric looked at Annette closely. He could see the pain. The long-ago dream shattered. "Let's give it a try," he said softly, reaching for her hand. As they reached the dance floor, the band had started to play a slow number. Eric took Annette into his arms. Her breath caught. His arms were strong, yet gentle. She felt her heart beat faster. She closed her eyes. She felt protected. Eric was an excellent dancer. They moved around the floor as one. She gave herself to the beat of the music, drifting, content. She felt his lips brush the top of her head. She looked up and focused on his face, his eyes. Those incredible velvet brown eyes! He held her closer as the music came to an end. They stood together, not moving.

Suddenly the band began playing a fast number. Eric grabbed her hand. "Come on, let's do it," he shouted. They danced. He was easy to follow, and they danced until they were breathless. Laughing and trying to catch their breath, they went back to the table. "You're a terrific dancer," Eric said.

"Thanks. So are you," Annette responded. "That was fun. I

haven't danced like that in a long time." She picked up her glass of ice water and took a swallow. Her heart was slowly returning to normal, but not completely. She had felt the reaction when he had taken her into his arms. She knew there was an attraction there. She had felt it before, but had tried to ignore it. But now there was no doubt. The band started again. Another slow tune. Eric glanced at her.

"Let's go try this one," he said, rising from his chair. He took her hand.

"Sure," Annette said, smiling. She felt her heartbeat increase again. They began dancing. Eric looked down at her. His eyes caressed her face. He wanted to kiss her. But he wasn't sure. She smiled up at him. After a few moments the music ended, but he held her hand as they waited for the band to begin another song. They danced the rest of the evening.

As the last song started, Eric held Annette closely. They were swaying to the music, their eyes closed. the last few notes of the refrain faded.... They stood motionless. Annette turned her head. Eric leaned down and gave her a soft lingering kiss on the lips. She looked somewhat startled. He hoped he hadn't done the wrong thing.

Slowly they walked back to their table and sat down. Annette felt somewhat shaken. She took a swallow of her Amaretto. The glass was almost empty. "Looks like they're about ready to close up," Eric said. The waiters were clearing off the final tables. Mario set the bill on the table in front of Eric. "I hope you enjoyed your evening," he said brightly. "It was a pleasure to serve you."

Annette excused herself to go to the ladies' room. "I'll take care of the bill and meet you at the entrance," Eric said.

"Okay," Annette said, as she headed for the lounge. She wanted to catch her breath and fix her lipstick. He had kissed her. She had sort of expected it. But she wasn't prepared for her reaction. Just the touch of his lips had triggered feelings that she wasn't ready for.

They drove to her apartment. He held her hand. At his touch she felt a tug at her heart. There certainly was a physical attraction here, she thought. "I had a terrific time tonight, Annette," Eric said softly.

"So did I," she replied with sincerity. She had enjoyed herself more than she thought she would.

"I'd like to see you again." He paused. "Do you like picnics?"

"A picnic?" she asked, half laughing. "Sure."

"Great," he said smiling. "How about next Sunday afternoon? I'll bring some cheese and wine and rolls..."

"And I can make a salad," Annette added.

"I know this really nice place up in the mountains, overlooking the valley," Eric said. "It's perfect for a picnic."

"It sounds great," Annette said, with a smile.

Eric turned toward her. "I'm looking forward to Sunday," he said.

Annette felt her heart start to gallop again. "So am I," she said, with a catch in her voice. She wondered if he was going to kiss her again. He leaned towards her and took her face in his hands. She closed her eyes. Slowly and gently he kissed her forehead, her eyes, the tip of her nose and her cheeks. She held her breath, and opened her eyes. He touched her lips gently with his fingertip then traced half circles on her cheekbones with his thumbs. The passions were stirring in her. She wanted more. But she was afraid, too. Not of him, the man, but of being hurt. She tried to keep a tight rein on her emotions. Until she was sure of him, whoever he was, and of herself, she would have to wait. But it was hard to do with Eric.

Eric felt his physical attraction for Annette growing. He wanted her very much, but it was too soon. He wasn't sure of her. He didn't want to move too fast. He had to proceed with caution, he thought. Especially since she had been hurt by his brother. But he really liked her, and wanted to get closer to her.

"I don't know what there is about you," she said to him, in a low voice. "But I feel that I've known you for a hundred years."

"I've felt that way ever since we met," Eric said, quietly. "It seemed like we'd known each other for a long time. I was so comfortable with you. And after the accident, when you came to the hospital to see me, it was the same way. You're quite a woman, Annette."

Hearing those words, Annette decided it was time to go in. She really wanted to stay here with him. She felt a comfort and closeness she hadn't felt with anyone for a long time, even more than with Herb. "I'd better go in, Eric. It's getting late," she said, somewhat reluctantly.

He glanced at his watch. It was hard to see the time in the dim light, but he knew it must be after two o'clock. "Okay, pretty lady," he said. He went around to her side of the car and opened the door for her. They walked across the grass and up the stairs to her apartment. She turned the key in the lock. The door swung open. She turned to face him. He hesitated. He put his arms around her. She could smell faintly the aroma of his cologne. His arms felt strong, safe.

"Thanks for a wonderful time, Eric," she said, smiling up at him. "I haven't had such an enjoyable evening for a long time."

"Neither have I, Annette," Eric said sincerely. "I'll give you a call during the week."

"Okay. Goodnight, Eric."

He leaned down. His eyes caressed her face. He brushed her lips lightly with his. "Goodnight, Annette," he said tenderly.

Annette went into her apartment and closed the door. She leaned against it. The awakened passions stirred within her. He made her feel alive, wanted. She hadn't felt like this in a long, long time. She looked at the single red rose that he had brought her earlier. It was a symbol of love!

The week passed, but slowly. Annette found herself unable to concentrate on even simple things. She was waiting for Sunday when she would see him again. He had called her. They had talked for hours. She couldn't get enough of his voice. His words caressed her. There was something about this man! Sherry heard about the evening. She was concerned for Annette. She didn't want her friend to be hurt again. And this time it could be the other brother! In the back of her mind Annette knew she should proceed with caution, but she was optimistic. She was intrigued by this man, and she felt he was attracted to her. Either that, or he was a very good actor!

The thought of Annette permeated Eric's waking moments. She was a special woman. He really liked her. He wanted to be with her. He wanted to make love to her, tenderly, lovingly. But it was too soon. He felt he had to handle this situation very carefully. He knew, even though perhaps unfairly, he was suspect because of his brother's actions. It would be hard to gain her trust, but she was worth it. He felt as if he had known her for a long, long time, and he wanted to know her better!

7

A gorgeous sunrise greeted Annette. She awoke to find the alarm clock on the floor. *Today is the day I will see Eric,* she thought happily. The phone rang.

"Good morning," he said cheerfully. There was a huskiness to his voice that made her heart skip. "Isn't it a great day for a picnic?"

"Hi, good morning," she responded with a smile in her voice.

"It's perfect!"

"What time shall I pick you up?" he inquired. "It'll take about an hour and a half to drive to the mountains."

"How about eleven?"

"Okay," he said. "By the way, I'm bringing some Swiss cheeses and some ham. I've also got rolls, and a bottle of wine that I think you'll enjoy."

"Ummm, sounds good," Annette responded. "I made some macaroni salad, too."

"All right!" Eric exclaimed. "I love that."

"Okay, see you soon," she said, glancing at the clock.

A few hours later Annette heard the doorbell ring. She opened the door. Eric stood there tall and smiling. He came towards her and enveloped her in his arms. "Hi, pretty lady," he said, holding her a moment longer.

"Hi yourself," she responded. She liked the feel of being in his embrace.

"Ready to go?"

"Just about. I've got the salad and stuff in the kitchen."

"Okay, I'll take them down to the car," he said, following her through the living room and into the kitchen. He gathered up the paper bags that were on the counter and carried them down the steps to his car. She closed and locked her apartment door, and went down the steps to meet him. He held the door open for her and closed it. Then he went around to his side of the car.

He was surprised to find she had opened his door slightly for him. That was a gesture women generally didn't make, at least the ones he had come into contact with. How considerate, he thought. "Thanks," he said, smiling at her.

She looked at him. Those incredible eyes again. That day they were sparkling, deep brown. They were two pools of velvet! She felt her heart jump.

The narrow mountain roads to the picnic spot wound through areas of forest. The scenery was breathtaking. Silver boulders dotted the landscape. A patchwork quilt of sunlight wove golds and greens around them. In the distance, snow sparkled on the tops of the mountains. After an hour or so they arrived at the top of the hill. The view was spectacular. Eric drove into a parking area and stopped. He turned to Annette. "Well, what do you think?" he asked her.

She couldn't believe it. It was almost like being on top of the world. The valley lay before them, green and velvety. A meadow behind them beckoned, daisies and other wildflowers bobbed in the summer afternoon breeze. There was a cleared area, surrounded by evergreen trees, perfect for a picnic. The jagged peaks of the Colorado Rockies stood majestically guarding the plateau. Capped in silver-white, they glistened in the afternoon sun.

"Oh Eric, it's wonderful," Annette cried. She opened the car door and stood transfixed, gazing at the surroundings. "How did you ever find this place?"

"Um, I had some help," he replied. He thought back to several years ago, when he'd first been here. It was with his sweetheart, Mary Ann. They had been inseparable, then she had run off with his best friend. His heart had ached for a long time. He hadn't wanted to come here again, until now. "I first came here with someone a long time ago," he said quietly, "and somehow I just never forgot it."

"I can see why," Annette said. "It's a place that no one could ever forget," she added, drinking in the beauty of what she saw.

Eric seemed pleased. "I'm glad you like it here." He got out of the car and came to stand next to her. "It's a place where you can get away from the pressures and stress of the world. It makes your problems seem very insignificant when you're so close to Nature and God."

She glanced at his face. She was glad that he had wanted to share this place with her. It was like a special bond. She felt so, anyway. She wondered if he did. There seemed to be a wistful look in his eyes.

"Well, shall we unload the car?" he inquired.

Together they carried the picnic items over to a grassy spot, and set the food and utensils on the tablecloth that Eric had brought. He picked up the bottle of wine, and expertly eased the cork from the bottle. Annette watched as he poured the blush-colored liquid into two long stemmed glasses. He gave one to her. Their hands touched for an instant, and she felt a current run through her. She looked up at him. Their eyes met and held. His expression was intent, searching.

"We should have a toast," he said, clearing his throat. "To a special place, special moments, and very special company." Their glasses met briefly, and they drank together. This was a beginning, of sharing, of special times. She felt it, and so did he. After they both had eaten their fill and consumed most of the wine, Eric asked Annette if she'd like to take a walk.

"That would be great," she answered with a grin. "We'd better put this stuff away first, however."

"Good idea," Eric said. "We don't want any unwelcome visitors."

Annette laughed. She picked up the picnic basket and carried it to the car. Eric gathered the tablecloth up and folded it. "I've got a blanket in the trunk," he said. "Why don't we take it with us so we can sit down on the ground and be comfortable?"

"Okay," Annette said, walking towards the edge of the hill.

He got the blanket out of the trunk and made sure the car was locked. He looked over at Annette. She was looking out at the valley. The wind was playing with her hair. It had grown longer, and shone golden in the sunlight. Her body was slender, firm. He could see the outline of her breasts against the thin cotton of her blouse. Her hips were outlined in her snug fitting jeans. He had noticed her figure before, but not like this. He walked slowly over to her and he put his arm around her slim waist and he drew her near to him. She put her arm around him, and together they walked slowly towards the meadow.

Above them the sky was crystal blue. Summer flowers nodded in the warm breeze. A palette of colors spread across the fields. After a while, Eric stopped and looked around. They were surrounded by the beauty of nature. "Why don't we sit down for a while?" he said. "This looks like a good spot. Underneath this tree," he gestured towards a large, sturdy tree trunk.

"Okay," Annette agreed. "My legs are sort of tired." She helped him spread the blanket on the grass. He sat down and leaned back against the smooth bark. She sat down next to him. "This place is absolutely beautiful," she said, glancing around her. The sunlight touching the leaves made them softly golden. She had been wondering about Eric's past. He never seemed to talk about it. She wanted to know more about him. He was somewhat mysterious. But she was hesitant to pry too much. She really liked him and respected him. She felt very comfortable with him, and she was finding the physical attraction growing.

"Are you from this area, Eric?" she gently asked.

"No, actually I was born in California. I lived there for quite a while," he answered.

"Was your brother born there, too?"

He hesitated. "Herb was, but I had another brother, Ted, who was born here in Colorado. He died in an auto accident about a year ago. We were really close to each other. It was quite a blow. My parents still haven't gotten over it." He paused. "Ted and I were much closer than Herb and I have ever been. He was quite a guy."

Annette looked up at Eric's face. She could see in his eyes the grief of losing someone dear. "I'm sorry," she said softly.

Eric glanced away briefly. His eyes were moist. "Ted really cared about people," he continued, "and people liked him. He was my older brother. I looked up to him ever since I was a kid. I miss him a lot." Eric swallowed, and cleared his throat. He hadn't shared things like this with anyone for a long time. He began playing with a leaf that had fallen. He twirled it in his fingers. "Herb is a little younger than me," he continued. "He's an okay guy, but sometimes he plays games with people. He doesn't really mean to hurt anyone, but he just doesn't always think how it will affect someone else. I guess you found that out yourself." Eric paused. "He even had his name changed to Edwards, because he thought it sounded more professional."

"Oh, that's why your last names are different," Annette exclaimed.

"Yes. I never could understand why he did it, and our folks couldn't either. They were hurt at first. It was as if their name wasn't good enough for him." Eric shook his head. "Herb's always trying to impress people."

Annette nodded. "I noticed that," she said, quietly.

"Herb is a very jealous person, Annette. He's very possessive," Eric said suddenly, "and he has a temper, especially when he's been drinking. I'm afraid that one of these days he's going to hurt someone. I try to calm him down when he gets that way, but sometimes he just won't listen."

Annette thought to herself how fortunate she was that she'd never seen Herb act that way. She could see how he might get out of control while he was drinking. And she knew he was possessive. He had shown that trait while they were dating. She was now glad their relationship had ended. And she was even more glad she had met Eric.

The afternoon passed, and they talked easily. He asked her about her family and places she had lived, what jobs she'd had, and about the auto accident that had ended her dancing career before it even started. They talked about their college years, and discussed their work and goals and possible future plans. But neither of them asked about past loves or lovers. It seemed better not to. He didn't ask about her relationship with Herb, which she was glad about. Only briefly had he mentioned Mary Ann, who had once been an important part of his life. But Annette didn't want to know about her. It was as though she and Eric were starting from the beginning. They had actually started several months ago, at Crystal Hill, but the past wasn't all that important. It had happened. It had brought them to where they were. But this was the here and now. That was what mattered.

The sun began to sink lower in the sky. "Are you getting cold?" Eric inquired.

"No, not yet," Annette replied. She smiled at him. She leaned back against the trunk of the big tree. He sat a short distance from her. Then he moved closer. He leaned towards her and gently caressed her hair. Her soft, green eyes focused on his face.

"You have beautiful eyes," he said.

Annette smiled. "Thanks," she said. "I feel so at peace here with you," she added, looking down at the ground.

"I'm glad," he answered. "I feel the same way. As I've said before, you're quite a woman, Annette." His eyes were serious. He took her face between his hands. His look caressed her. He lowered his head slowly and found her lips with his. Gently at first, then more deeply. "I've wanted to kiss you like this for a long time," he said breathlessly.

She returned his kiss with passion and sweetness. They embraced. He wanted to kiss her again. She ran her fingers down the back of his neck, and felt the hard muscles of his shoulder.

"Oh, Annette," he breathed into her ear. She had never felt such a strong physical reaction to any man like this before. The intensity they felt grew stronger. He held her tightly. The undertow beckoned. It would be easy to let herself go with the tide of passion she felt. Very easy. But it was not what she wanted. Not yet, not here. She wanted that moment to be special, and a commitment.

Eric touched her face tenderly. She looked up at him. Traces of tears were in her eyes. "I'm falling in love with you, Annette," he said slowly. "I've felt it for quite a while. I've wanted to tell you. But I was kind of afraid. I guess I wanted to be sure that you weren't still in love with Herb." He paused for a moment. "Herb seems to think that you are," he added.

Annette snuggled against Eric's arm. The air was getting chilly now, but she wasn't cold, not at all. He put his arm more firmly around her and lightly kissed her cheek. A furrow briefly crossed her forehead. "Eric," she said, looking directly into his eyes, "my relationship with Herb has been over for a long time, no matter what he says." She paused. "I've felt attracted to you, too, from the beginning. But I was afraid to get involved. I didn't want to be hurt again."

His eyes searched her face. "I'll try never to hurt you, Annette," he said to her. He gently brushed a few strands of her hair back from her forehead. "I really care about you."

She smiled at him. She gazed deeply into his eyes. Those incredible velvet brown eyes. They embraced. "We found out a lot about each other today," she said. "I'm so glad we came up here. It brought us so much closer."

"Yes, it did. I'm glad we came here, too, Annette. But I think it's about time to go back to the car," he said, somewhat reluctantly. The sun was casting long shadows on the ground. The evening air was getting cooler. He helped her to her feet. She looked at him in wonderment. They had reached a new plateau in their relationship. They had crossed a bridge. He took her hand, and together they headed toward the car. Dusk was approaching. A star appeared in the deep azure sky above. It looked down and winked unseen at the man and woman walking hand in hand.

8

One evening, several weeks after the picnic, Annette was at her apartment when the doorbell rang. She knew it wasn't Eric; he was away for a few days on a business trip. Thinking it was the paper boy, she reached for her purse and took out her billfold. The doorbell rang again. She opened the door, expecting to see his tall, lanky form. Instead, a different sight greeted her. She dropped her wallet in astonishment! Her breath caught in her throat. She couldn't believe it. There stood Herb! Her mouth fell open. She started to speak, but he interrupted her.

"Surprised?" Herb said. He had a devious grin, and had obviously been drinking. "Well, aren't you going to ask me in?"

Annette swallowed hard. "Herb, if you're looking for Eric, he's not here," she said, bending down to retrieve her wallet.

"Naw, I'm not looking for Eric. He's out of town. I know tha-a-at," he stammered. "I came to see youuu."

Annette was trembling. . . . She had never seen him this way. Eric's words about how Herb acted when he was drunk echoed in her head. Before she could react, he pushed his way inside the door.

"Herb, you're drunk," Annette said, disgustedly. "You should go home. We can talk another time."

He wheeled around. "So I've been drinking. So what?" he sneered. "Whatsamatter, I'm not good enough for you, is that it?"

Annette looked at him. "What are you talking about?" she shouted.

"Oh, I know about you. You've been makin' it with my brother." He staggered towards the kitchen. Annette followed him. She thought maybe some coffee would help.

"I'll fix you some coffee," she told Herb.

"I don't want any coffeeeee," he slurred. "I want you." He moved towards her. There was a wild look in his eyes. Annette knew she had to be careful with him. Eric had said Herb had a bad temper when he was drinking, and she didn't want him to unleash it on her. "Herb, why don't you sit down and take it easy," she said, stepping away from him. She took the coffee can in her hands, and started to spoon coffee into the filter.

"How could you do this to me?" he shouted, glaring at her.

"Do what?"

"How could you go with my brother when I still love you?"

Annette was stupefied. "What?" she said.

"I still love you, Annette," he said loudly. "I've always loved you." His gaze narrowed. "You still love me. I know you do. And I still love you. I want you." He staggered towards her.

Annette was scared. She was no match physically for him, even though he was intoxicated. And he was in no mood for talking!

"Herb," she began, "I think you misunderstand. I'm not in love with you any more. You love Helen. Why don't you go home to your wife and..."

Her sentence went unfinished. He lunged towards her and grabbed her shoulders hard. The open coffee can went flying across the counter. Coffee went in all directions. "I know what you're doing, you little bitch," he said, shaking her roughly. "You're seeing Eric to make me jealous." He was in a rage. All the pent-up emotion, frustration and jealousy that had built up within him for months, now had an outlet—her. He slapped her hard across the face. Once, Twice. Again! Annette screamed and covered her face with her hands.

"Herb, that's not true," she cried, shaking her head. "Please, listen to me."

"Why should I listen to you?" he yelled. "Whatever you say is a lie, anyhow." He lunged for her again. Annette was terrified. She moved towards the doorway, but he was too quick for her. He caught her arm and pulled her roughly to him. She smelled his breath close to her face. He reeked of whiskey. He tried to kiss her. She turned her head away and pushed hard against him. She felt her shirt tear. Despite being drunk, he had incredible strength. "Helen left me," he shouted at her. "She took the kid and left."

Annette tried to wrestle free. "I'm sorry, Herb, I really am," she said, trying to catch her breath. "But why are you doing this?" she cried. Tears were streaming down her face.

"Becaauuse I love you, Annette," he stuttered. "And I waannt you. If I can't have you, no one else is going to have you. Eschpecially my brother!" She saw the look of rage in his eyes. This man was the one she had once loved. Unbelievable! Now he was totally out of control. He was dangerously unreasonable, and she was frightened for her life!

Herb looked down for an instant and Annette saw her chance and broke free. She ran into the living room. He came after her. She tried to head for the door. He was close behind her. She was desperate. She looked for some kind of weapon to protect herself, to slow him down. Anything. She saw a ceramic vase on the table and reached for it. Herb came up behind her and grabbed her arm. She struggled with him. He savagely twisted her arm. She grimaced with pain, but somehow was able to get the vase with her other hand. She hit him on the shoulder. But it was a glancing blow. She screamed and tried to run.

"You bitch," he shouted, as he viciously backhanded her. She cried out. The force of the blow sent her reeling. As she fell, she felt something hard and sharp strike her forehead. Blinding pain. She almost blacked out. Something warm began trickling down her face. Blood, she thought, faintly. She lay on the floor, gasping for breath. If only Eric were here. He'd know how to handle Herb. But he wasn't, and she was alone in this. She was almost afraid to move, for fear he would hit her again, or try to kill her. But she was also afraid she may pass out, and then be at his mercy. She didn't know what he would do next, but she was determined to survive, even if it took every last ounce of her physical strength!

Herb was unaware how hard he had actually hit Annette. When he saw her fall and her head hit the coffee table, he began to sober up. His anger started to subside and he began to feel remorse. Blood was coming from her forehead, soaking into her blonde hair. He must have really hurt her, he thought. He hadn't meant to. He loved her. His head ached. The alcohol was wearing off, and here he was with the woman he still loved. He had physically hurt her. What was the matter with him? He walked over to where she lay and bent over her. She cringed. She reached out and felt his shoe near her. She recoiled, terrified!

"Don't hit me again, Herb, please," she sobbed.

He touched the blood on her forehead. Her face was beginning to swell from the blows he had imposed on her. "Oh, God, Annette," he said, his voice shaking. "I didn't mean to hurt you. I love you." He knelt next to her. "I'm sorry ... I'm so sorry," he murmured, holding his face in his hands. He took her in his arms and cradled her. His eyes filled with tears.

Annette's whole body ached terribly. She became dimly aware that Herb was holding her. She wanted to get away. He was crazy, she thought. He wanted to kill her, or rape her. She knew she had to get away from him, and find medical help. Somehow. "Don't touch me," she shouted, pushing away from him. She rolled towards the table. "I hate you. Get out of here. Go. I never want to see you again. Get out, do you hear me?" she shrieked. Her whole body was shaking.

"But you need help, Annette. You need to go to a doctor. I'll take you."

"No, you're the one that needs help, Herb," she said, between swollen lips. "I don't want you to do anything for me. Ever! Now will you get the hell out of here before I call the police and have you thrown out and locked up?"

Herb got up slowly. He was dazed. The vase lay in several pieces near his foot. He picked them up and set them on the table. He looked at the woman who sat on the floor, bleeding, and bruised. He shook his head. Tears came to his eyes. He slowly walked over to the door. "I'm so sorry," he said again, as he opened it, and then left.

As soon as she saw the door close, Annette crawled to the couch. Her head felt like it would explode. With sheer determination, she painfully raised herself up on the cushions. She picked up the phone and dialed Sherry's number. Please let her be there, she prayed.

"Hullo," came the somewhat sleepy voice over the phone.

Annette took a deep breath. Even that hurt a lot. "Sherry, it's Annette," she mumbled. "I need some help."

"Annette, what's wrong?"

"Well, I had a little problem tonight, and I need to go to the emergency room."

Sherry suddenly came awake. "Oh no, what happened?"

Annette didn't want to go into all the details. She was hurting. Bad. And just wanted to go to the hospital. "I sort of had a fight with Herb," she said, her voice filled with tears. "He was drunk!"

"Oh my God, Annette. I'll be right there!"

"Thanks, I owe you one." Annette hung up the phone and gingerly got up. She staggered to the bathroom and looked in the mirror. The image that looked back at her was a stranger. The ugly cut on her forehead had stopped bleeding, but streaks of red remained in her hair and on her face. The area around the wound was beginning to swell. Bruises were beginning to appear around her eyes and on her cheeks. Her lips were swollen. Her shirt was torn, and her arm was turning black and blue where Herb had twisted it. She looked like she had been in a gang fight, and the other guys had won. She turned on the cold water and held a washcloth under it. Then put it to her puffy, bruised face. Incredible pain. She closed her eyes, and the tears began.

Sherry arrived at Annette's apartment a few minutes later. She gasped when Annette opened the door. Even in the dim light she could see her bruised, swollen face and cut forehead. She gave her a brief hug. Tears trickled down Annette's face. "Oh, Sherry, this has been a nightmare," she sobbed. "Herb tried to kill me!"

"Come on, let's get you to the hospital," Sherry said, as she helped Annette on with her jacket. She closed the apartment door, took her friend's arm, and helped her down the stairs to the car. Shortly after they left, the phone started ringing in Annette's apartment. It was a few minutes after eleven.

"What on earth happened?" Sherry asked, as they drove to the hospital.

"It was unreal," Annette mumbled. It was difficult for her to talk. "Herb came over. He was drunk and angry that Eric and I are seeing each other. He said he still loved me, then he went crazy and started yelling and hitting me. I tried to defend myself, and he got madder. I fell against the table, I guess. I think that sobered him up because then he said he was sorry and wanted to take me to a doctor... I don't know. The whole thing is so bizarre..."

Sherry glanced at Annette. "It looks like he really beat you up badly. Are you going to press charges against him?"

Annette looked down at her trembling hands. "I don't know. I'm kind of afraid to," she said, her voice shaking.

"How are you going to tell Eric about this?"

"I don't know," she said again. "If I tell him what really happened, he might try and kill Herb. Or Herb might try and hurt Eric. Knowing how Herb lies, he might tell Eric that I encouraged him." She paused. "I don't want him to know. I'll just tell him I fell down the steps, or something."

"Annette, he's going to find out the truth, sometime. It's possible that Herb might feel guilty and tell him himself. Then what?"

Annette sighed. "Yeah, I suppose that could happen," she said slowly. "I tried to reason with him, Sherry. I told him to leave me alone and that I didn't love him anymore. I also told him to go home to his wife and kid. He said that Helen had taken the child and left. He kept saying that he loved me, and that he was sure I loved him too. The man is crazy, Sherry. And he is insanely jealous of his brother."

Sherry shook her head. "I still think Eric should know what his brother did to you. Who knows, Annette, he might try to hurt you again."

"I don't think so. He was really drunk, Sherry. I've never seen him like that before. When we were on the picnic, Eric told me Herb really has a temper when he's been drinking, and sometimes it gets out of hand. He was right. But he also said Herb doesn't really mean to hurt anyone."

"Yeah, right," Sherry offered, "just look at you!"

Annette fell silent. They pulled into the emergency room entrance. Sherry stopped the car and got out. Annette tried to open her door with her uninjured arm. She was really aching all over now, and her head hurt unbearably. She felt somewhat dizzy. Sherry came around to her side of the car and helped her get out. She put her arm around her and together they walked through the double doors to the waiting area. There were a couple of other people in the room. The lady at the reception desk glanced at them, and offered them a seat at the desk. The cut on Annette's head had started bleeding again. The receptionist produced some forms, and asked questions. A few minutes later, a doctor appeared. He asked for Annette Howard. She rose and began to follow him down a hallway.

He turned towards her. "What happened to you?" he asked.

"I fell down some steps," she answered.

Sherry sat in the waiting room. She glanced at the clock on the wall. It was 12:30 a.m. Annette had been with the doctor for about a half hour. It seemed like an eternity. She flipped through an old magazine. A few minutes later the doctor appeared. He walked over to her and introduced himself as Dr. Anderson. He told her that her friend had a possible concussion, and multiple cuts and bruises. He also said she should be kept overnight for observation. Sherry listened earnestly. The doctor wanted to know how she had gotten hurt. It appeared to him that someone had beaten her. Sherry responded that she didn't really know what had happened. Just that Annette had said she had fallen and hurt her head, and wanted Sherry to take her to the hospital.

The doctor nodded. "I think we'd better admit her," he said gently. "She has suffered quite a few injuries."

"All right," Sherry said quietly. "I'll come and see how she is tomorrow. Thanks, Dr. Anderson."

"You're welcome. It's a good thing you brought her in here tonight," he said.

Eric had tried to phone Annette several times. The last time was about midnight. He had gotten out of his meeting late, and hadn't had a chance to call her until after 11:00. There had been no answer. He thought that was kind of strange, especially on a week night. Maybe she had to work late? Or maybe she and some friends had gone out somewhere. But she wouldn't be this late getting home, he thought. For some reason he was concerned. He looked at the clock on the dresser. It was 1:15 a.m. He called her again. No answer. I'll call her in the morning, he thought. Maybe she was asleep and just didn't hear the phone, and had forgotten to turn on the answering machine.

Annette awoke in an unfamiliar place. Her head was throbbing mercilessly. She slowly looked around her. It was an effort to even blink. The walls were white. She was in a strange bed. It took a few moments to remember last night. It seemed ages ago: She remembered Herb's drunken rage, Sherry bringing her here, and the doctor saying that she should stay for observation. And now, here she was. What now?

A nurse appeared and cheerfully said, "Good morning."

Annette tried to smile, but her mouth hurt. Her lips felt like straw. She glanced down. Her right arm was heavily bandaged, and there were bruises on her left one. She felt like someone had hit her with at least twenty baseball bats. Her head felt like it weighed a ton. There were noises at the doorway. She looked up and saw the tall, slender form of Dr. Anderson coming briskly across the room. His face grew serious as he reached for her wrist and took her pulse.

"How do you feel this morning?" he inquired.

"Sort of like I've been used for batting practice," Annette joked.

"I'm not surprised," the doctor said. "You have a possible concussion with cuts and multiple bruises. That must have been quite a fall!"

Annette looked away. "Yeah, it was," she said. "As I recall, I think my head hit the corner of a table."

Dr. Anderson looked closely at Annette's bruised and swollen face. "I'd say that from the nature and extent of your injuries, you were a victim of a beating," he said, with concern in his voice.

She turned her face away. "I guess it's not easy to hide it from a doctor," she said. Tears were welling in her eyes. "Okay, a friend of mine got drunk and lost control," she said slowly. "I was embarrassed to admit it. He's never done anything like that before." She paused. "He just got upset and took it out on me."

Dr. Anderson smiled down at her. "It's okay, Annette. I thought from the beginning that someone had hit you. Even though you said you had fallen down some steps. When someone gets drunk and out of control, they can possess unbelievable strength. Unfortunately, you discovered that yourself."

Annette slowly nodded her head. "I guess so," she said. She felt somewhat dizzy. "How long do I have to stay here?" she asked.

"Well, it depends," the doctor answered. "We're going to take X-rays. I think you may have a concussion. Depending on the results, you may be able to leave later on today. Do you have anyone to look after you at home?"

"Well, not in my apartment. I have friends nearby, but no roommate," she answered.

"Okay, let's see how things go, and we'll decide what is the best thing to do," the doctor said. He checked the wound on her forehead and her other injuries, then left the room.

Annette gingerly laid her head down on the pillow and closed her eyes. How was she going to tell Eric about this? He would be back in a few days. She could tell him she had fallen down some steps, or had tripped and fallen in her apartment. She couldn't tell him what really happened. She just couldn't! But she didn't want to lie, either!

9

Eric tried to call Annette when he awoke the next morning. It was 6 a.m. Early, yes, but he wanted to be sure she was all right. There was no answer. He was truly puzzled. Maybe she had spent the night with a girlfriend? It was a work day. He'd try and call her at work later. Maybe her phone was out of order at the apartment. He tried to think positively, but there was a nagging feeling inside him that something was wrong.

Sherry awoke to the piercing ring of the alarm clock. She was exhausted. It had been a short night. She showered and dressed. She wasn't really hungry for breakfast. She was concerned about Annette, and wanted to get to work early. She'd have to tell Annette's supervisor that she wouldn't be in today. After some thought, she decided to say that Annette had had a fall, and wasn't feeling well. That was partially true, she thought. She wouldn't say anything that Annette wouldn't want her to say. Later on she'd call the hospital and see how she was doing.

Eric's meeting started at 8:00 sharp. He had wanted to call Annette's apartment again, before he went in, but was unable to do so since some of his business associates had invited him to breakfast. When they had a break at 10:30, he'd call her at work.

"Good morning, Smith & Wheeler Advertising," the cheerful voice replied.

"Good morning, I'd like to speak to Annette Howard."

"One moment, please," the voice responded.

"Design and Copy," an unfamiliar voice answered.

"I'd like to speak to Annette Howard, please."

"I'm sorry, but Annette is out sick. Can someone else help you?" The words echoed in Eric's head. "She's out sick?" he repeated.

"That's right. Are you calling about a specific ad campaign?"

"No, no, I was just trying to get hold of Annette. I'm calling long distance."

"Oh, I see. Well she's not here today. Would you like to leave a message, in case she calls in?"

Eric hesitated. "No," he said, then changed his mind. "Well, maybe I will, after all. Please tell her that Eric Woodward called from Chicago. I'm staying at the Concord Hotel, Room 519. She can reach me there until Friday night. I'll try to get in touch with her at home later. Thanks."

"You're welcome, sir. Thank you for calling."

Eric hung up the receiver. He was mystified. Where was she? It wasn't like her to just take off from work. She must have called in sick. But from where? Why wasn't she at home? He called the long distance operator and asked her to check the number at Annette's apartment, that he had been having difficulty getting through. There was no trouble with the number, he was told. Now what? He wanted to run to the airport and catch the next plane for Denver. Now. But he still had three days to go until the meetings ended. He was getting very concerned about Annette. He wondered if something had happened to her. Too many things didn't add up.

Annette's X-rays confirmed that she had a slight concussion and cracked ribs. When greeted with this news, she was not surprised. She felt like her whole head had been filled with concrete, and someone had tried to drill holes in it. Each time she took a deep breath, it felt like a knife was slicing into her side. Dr. Anderson was concerned about her condition and had asked another doctor to come and see her. His name was Dr. Weller, and he was energetic and pleasant. He told Annette that she shouldn't be left alone for any length of time, because of her head injury, and the medication they had to give her. Together the two doctors convinced her to stay in the hospital for another day or two until she could make arrangements to stay with someone. Sherry came to visit Annette several times. During the last visit, Annette told her that the doctors wanted her to stay in the hospital a couple of more days, but after that they didn't want her to be alone.

"Annette, you can stay with me," Sherry offered. "I can pick you up Friday night, and you can stay with me over the weekend. Then, depending on how you feel, I can either take you home, or over to my sister Ann. She'd love to have you stay with her."

"Thanks, but I don't want to be a bother," Annette groaned.

"Don't be silly, you're not," Sherry replied. "Besides, I'm pretty good at playing nurse."

Annette smiled faintly. "Florence Nightingale, I suppose," she quipped.

Sherry laughed. "Of course. I'll talk to your doctor and see if it's okay."

All right, if you're sure."

"I'm sure. Don't worry about it. I've got a nice guest room, lots of food, TV, cassettes and CD's, all the comforts of home. And you can get lots of rest."

Annette looked hard at her friend. "Thanks," she said, feeling the tears gathering in back of her eyes. "You're great."

Sherry leaned over and gave her a hug. "We'll get through this," she said. "It's going to be okay." She felt so badly for her friend. How could anyone do this to someone they supposedly cared about? She had heard about domestic violence, but had never known anyone who had experienced it, until now. "I've got to be going," she said. "I'll call you tomorrow and see how you're doing."

"All right," Annette replied. "Thanks again. Sherry."

Eric tried to call Annette one more time. He got the same response. No answer. She hadn't returned his call from work, either. He had one more day in Chicago. Then he'd find out what was going on in Denver!

Sherry arrived at the hospital late Friday afternoon. She waited while Annette finished the release paperwork, and was taken, in a wheelchair to the side entrance. Then she helped her into her car and they headed for Sherry's apartment.

"How're you feeling?" Sherry inquired.

"Not too bad. My heads hurts off and on, but it feels a lot better than it did. Thank God the swelling has gone down in my face. At least now I don't look like a woman of the streets who has been beaten up by her pimp."

Sherry glanced over at Annette. "Or like someone who was in a fight with an ex-boyfriend, either."

Annette flushed. "I've never been beaten by anyone, ever. I had no idea how awful it could be."

Sherry cleared her throat. "Annette, what about Eric? He's probably been trying to call you and is wondering where you are."

Annette turned her face towards the window. "I know," she said quietly. She looked at the bumper-to-bumper rush hour traffic around them. "He had said he would call me from Chicago and tell me where he was staying, but I haven't been home to get the message, so I don't have a clue where he is or how to get in touch with him."

"When do you think he'll be coming back to Denver?" Sherry asked.

"I'm not sure. Tonight, or maybe tomorrow."

"Are you going to call him after he gets back?"

Annette paused and shut her eyes. The glare of the sunlight reflected off the red car in front of them was making her head hurt more. She reached in her purse for her sunglasses. "I don't know, Sherry," she said. "If I do, I'll have to explain why I haven't been around, and I don't know what to tell him yet."

Sherry sighed. "Annette, you've got to tell him the truth. You really care about each other. You can't jeopardize your relationship by lying. What his brother did to you is inexcusable. And this was not your fault. Herb needs help. He came on to you. He was drunk. You were trying to defend yourself. I somehow get the feeling that you think you're responsible for him doing this to you. That's nonsense, Annette. He's the one. He's the one that hurt you. And he's the one who should feel guilty."

Annette slowly shook her head. "I had no idea that he was so jealous of Eric. I know it's not my fault, Sherry. Herb can twist things around, and make it sound like I came on to him. And he can be very persuasive, and conniving."

"You don't really think that Eric would believe that, do you?"

"I don't know what to think right now," Annette said in a tired voice. "But it's going to take me a long time to forgive him," she said grimly as she removed her glasses and took a compact out of her purse. She grimaced at the black and blue patches around her eyes. They would take a long time to heal.

Sherry drove into the parking lot at the Castlewood Apartments. "Well, here we are," she said brightly. "Home, sweet home."

Flight 192 from Chicago was scheduled to arrive in Denver at 7:30 p.m., but was delayed 25 minutes due to turbulence. The wheels touched down, Eric glanced at his watch, and reached overhead for his carry-on bag. It was about 8:00. He had caught an earlier flight than planned. He was anxious to get to a telephone and call Annette. He collected his garment bag, deplaned and went into the terminal. Against a wall he saw a bank of telephones and headed for them. He picked up the receiver, then hesitated. No, he suddenly decided, as he hung up the phone. He wasn't going to call her. He was going to drive over to her apartment. He'd find out first hand what was going on.

It was about 9 p.m. when he drove into the parking lot of Annette's apartment building. He stopped the car and got out. Her car was in its parking space. He jogged up the stairs to her apartment. It was dark and eerily quiet. The curtains were drawn. There was no sign of life. He knocked and waited. Again. He rang the doorbell, but there was no response. He waited a few more minutes, then he turned and walked slowly down the steps. *Where could she be,* he wondered. As he turned to go back to his car, his eye caught her mailbox. There was something white sticking out of the top. He walked over to it. Mail was in there, stuffed inside. He glanced down. A large brown envelope rested against the wall. It was addressed to Annette Howard. It looked like it had been there for a while. Eric swallowed over the lump in his throat. Something had happened. He felt it. But what? Where was she? He was at a complete loss.

"I'll have to go over tomorrow and pick up some things," Annette said sleepily. "It's too late tonight."

Sherry folded back the covers on the guest room bed. "If you need anything, just let me know," she said, smiling at Annette. She sat on the edge of the bed.

Annette gingerly smiled back at her. Her mouth was still sore. "Thanks. I don't know what I'd do without you. We've been through a hell of a lot together, haven't we?"

Sherry nodded. "No one would ever believe it. Maybe we'll write a book together someday."

Annette chuckled. "Now that would be something different." She looked at the wall. "I don't know what I'm going to do, Sherry. I really don't."

Sherry got up. "Don't think about it tonight, Annette," she said with concern in her voice. "Just get some sleep, and we'll work on it tomorrow. Okay?"

"Okay," Annette agreed as Sherry reached to turn off the light. Annette was exhausted. It was too much to worry about now. She closed her eyes.

"Goodnight," Sherry said.

"Goodnight," Annette answered.

10

Herb paced up and down. He couldn't sleep. It was the third night of sleeplessness. He would doze for a while, then wake up from a nightmare, drenched in perspiration. He kept seeing her face. Blood. Bruises. A voice echoed from somewhere. "Why did you do this, you maniac?" He kept hearing screams, her screams. He hadn't meant to hurt her, but he had. He had no idea how much. He loved her. And his brother loved her. And she loved his brother! Damn! He couldn't let go. He had to tell Eric, somehow. But he was afraid. Maybe he could convince Eric that Annette had asked for it. That she had led him on. Maybe. But he doubted Eric would believe it. He had been drunk and had gotten out of control. It had happened before, but never to a woman they both cared about. He wondered if Annette would tell Eric. He was scared and confused. His wife had left him, and now he had no one. He didn't like that. He needed a drink.

Eric sat in the darkened living room. He had been watching TV, but had turned it off. He couldn't concentrate. Thoughts about Annette were swirling in his head. She had disappeared, vanished. She wasn't at home. She hadn't been at work. Her car was there. Mail was waiting for her. Surely, if she had gone on a spur of the moment trip, she would have had someone pick up her mail. He didn't know any of her friends, except for one—the woman he had met at Smith & Wheeler with Annette that day. What was her name? Sharon? No, Cherie? No. Sherry. That's it. Sherry something. He couldn't remember her last name. How many Sherry's could work there? He'd try and get ahold of her on Monday. Maybe she knew something about Annette. And tomorrow, he decided, he'd visit Annette's apartment manager. She must know something about where she was.

Mrs. Ames was completing her tour of the apartment buildings. It was early Saturday morning. She was collecting mail and packages that hadn't been picked up by the tenants. She had noticed quite a lot of mail in Apt. 17's mailbox. There was a large brown envelope addressed to Annette leaning against the wall. She checked the list of people on vacation. Howard wasn't among them. She went up to Annette's apartment. No response. The curtains were drawn and there was no activity. Well, she thought, Annette must have gone out of town and forgotten to call the office. She took the envelope to the manager's office and made a note to tell the mailman to bring the mail in Annette's box to the office. She would have him leave a message in the mailbox to let Annette know her mail had been picked up.

Eric drove into the parking lot of the Greenway Apartments. He drove slowly around to the Rental Office and parked in a "visitor" space. A glance at his watch showed it was about 9 a.m. The shades were open, and he walked to the entrance. An "Open" sign hung on the door. He entered the office where a middle-aged, energetic-looking woman sat at a desk. She looked up and smiled. "Can I help you?" she inquired.

"I hope so," Eric said as he slid into a chair. "I'm Eric Woodward, and I'm trying to get ahold of a friend of mine who lives here. Her name is Annette Howard, and she lives in Apt. 17." He cleared his throat. "I-I've been trying to contact her since last Tuesday, and there's been no answer," he continued. "I've been out of town on a business trip. I called her work number, and they said she was out sick. When I got in last night, I came here to see if she was home. Her car was here, but she didn't answer the door when I knocked. I also noticed her mail was still in her mailbox. I'm quite concerned. I wondered if she had left any information here as to where she might be." He looked pleadingly at the woman.

Erica Ames noticed the look of concern on Eric's face. She, too, wondered where her tenant of apartment seventeen was. She didn't want to upset this man, but she had to say something. "Mr. Woodward," she began, "I'm Erica Ames, the manager. I noticed the mail also, and picked it up this morning. Annette doesn't seem to be home, and I'm sorry, but I have no idea where she is either. Usually tenants notify us if they are going to be away. Annette has always done that in the past. I wish I could help you." She paused. "I'm sure she's fine. Probably had something unexpected come up. I wouldn't worry. I'm sure you'll hear from her soon."

Eric thanked her and left. Her gave her his phone number, just in case. In case of what? He didn't know. But he felt better anyway. Strange. She didn't even tell her apartment manager that she would be gone. She had always done that in the past. But why not now? He went up the stairs to her apartment, hoping. No response. He thought about knocking on her next-door neighbor's door. To see if she knew where Annette was, but on second thought decided against it.

Annette's next door neighbor, Susan Marks, hadn't seen Annette for several days. Ever since that night when she had heard loud crashing noises and banging and shouting. It had sounded like a fight of some sort. She didn't know Annette very well, though, and didn't want to get involved in a neighbor's problem. She thought she had seen a guy at Annette's door before it all started. Probably had a fight with her boyfriend. It's none of my business, anyway, she decided.

Annette awoke during the night, her head hurting badly. She got out of bed and went into the bathroom to take some pain pills. She turned the light on and looked in the mirror. Her bruised face stared back at her. She remembered how she had felt that night after Herb had left. What an awful night that was! She began to feel dizzy, and sat down on the lid of the toilet, resting her head in her hands. Tears began to stream down her cheeks, making her palms wet. A few minutes later Sherry appeared in the doorway. "Are you okay?" she asked.

"Yeah, I think so," Annette responded. "I woke up and my head hurt, so I came in here to take some pain pills. I just feel a bit woozy. Sorry I woke you."

"Hey, that's okay," Sherry said quickly. "I was just concerned about you." She saw the tears and handed Annette a tissue. "I know this is all really hard for you, Annette," she said gently.

"What time is it?" Annette inquired, wiping her eyes.

"About 2:30."

"Oh, I wish my head would stop hurting. I've never had such a headache in my life. God, Sherry, why did he do this to me?" she sobbed.

"I don't know, Annette. He's really a mixed-up guy. He needs help. It's a good thing you didn't marry him." She paused. "Why don't you try to get some sleep now?"

Eric spent the morning at the grocery store and the cleaners. Before he had left for Chicago, he and Annette had tentatively planned to get together for dinner at his apartment on Saturday night. Now it was Saturday and he had no idea where she was!

He stopped at his office to do a few things, and saw Herb's car in the parking lot. He must be catching up on some work, too, he thought. He went inside and walked down the hallway to his brother's office. Herb was at his desk. He was unshaven and looked as if he'd been through more than one rough night.

"Hi, bro," Eric called cheerily. "How's it going?"

Herb looked up. His brother was the last person he wanted to see. He didn't know what to say to him. Eric's manner seemed to imply that he didn't know what had happened to Annette. "Hi," Herb answered. "How was Chicago?"

"Fine. We had some good meetings," Eric said. "What have you been up to? Looks like you've been partying a bit."

"Yeah, a bit," Herb said, sarcastically. He ran his hand over his whiskered chin. He'd really been hitting the bottle the past few days, ever since that night. He couldn't get it out of his mind.

"Well, how about getting together tonight?" Eric asked.

Herb stared at his brother. No, he couldn't know anything about his fight with Annette. If he had, Herb would be up against the wall with Eric's fist in his face.

"Well, okay," Herb said tentatively. "I'm kind of surprised you'd ask, though. I thought you and Annette would be going out tonight."

At the mention of her name, Eric became suddenly depressed. "I thought so, too. But she's disappeared, Herb. It's really weird. She hasn't been home for days. I tried to call her at work. She wasn't there. Her apartment manager doesn't know where she is, either. I can't imagine what's happened to her."

"Aw, maybe she just decided to go visit someone, or go on vacation or something," Herb said warily. He was wondering himself now, where she'd gone.

"No, her vacation isn't scheduled for at least two months, Herb.

She wouldn't just take off and not let the manager know she was gone. I drove over to her apartment last night, after I got back. Her mail was still in the mailbox. Her car is there, but there's no sign of her. I'm really concerned."

Herb had heard enough. He was scared now and didn't want to say anything else. He didn't want to make any mistakes. "Oh, she's probably all right, Eric," he said with more conviction than he felt. "Don't worry about it. Women do funny things sometimes. Why don't you come over to my place for dinner? I've got some steaks we can barbecue, then maybe we'll go to a movie or something."

Eric nodded his head slowly. "Okay," he said without enthusiasm. "What time?"

"Seven-ish. Bring some beer if you want. I've got plenty of whiskey."

"Yes, I'll bet you do," Eric thought to himself. He was going to talk to his brother about his heavy drinking. Herb seemed to be doing more of it lately. "Okay, see you later," he said. "I've got some work to do, so I'd better get at it."

Sherry glanced at the clock on the dresser. It was 11:30 a.m. "We'd better get dressed and go over to your place and get your mail and the other things you need," she said to Annette.

"Yes. I want to check the answering machine, too. There's probably a ton of messages on it," Annette answered.

By the time they reached Annette's apartment complex, it was 12:30. The rental office had closed at noon. Sherry parked in front of Annette's apartment. "C'mon up with me while I get my things," she said to Sherry. "I'm still a bit unsteady."

"Oh, wait a minute," Sherry cried, "don't you want to check your mailbox first?"

"Sure, that'll just take a minute," Annette answered. She opened her mailbox. It was empty except for a note saying that, in her absence, her mail was being kept at the office. There was only one problem; the manager's office was closed now and wouldn't be open until Monday. Oh well, nothing she could do about that now. She should have called her apartment manager and told her she wouldn't be there for a while. Well, she'd take care of that on Monday.

Upon entering the apartment, Annette discovered, much to her horror, that she had forgotten to turn on the answering machine the night she went to the hospital. "Oh, no," she shouted, "I forgot to turn this thing on. Now I don't know who might have tried to call, though I'm sure Eric did."

Sherry looked at her. "You haven't been here for several days. No one knew where you were, except me. Everyone's probably wondering what happened to you."

Annette turned on the machine and sank down on the couch. Her glance caught the broken pieces of vase lying on the table. All of a sudden, memories of that terrifying night flooded over her. She closed her eyes and shuddered.

"This place smells like coffee," Sherry said. as she walked into the kitchen. "Oh my God, no wonder," she cried. "There's coffee all over the place!"

Annette heard Sherry's exclamation. She remembered that night vividly. Coffee. She had been trying to fix coffee for Herb, to sober him up. She slowly got to her feet, went to the kitchen doorway, and looked around. Ground coffee was scattered all over the floor, as well as the counter and table. A ten-pound, empty coffee can lay on its side amidst the mess. One of the kitchen chairs was turned over. A ceramic mug stood on the table, empty.

Sherry looked at Annette in amazement. "What on earth happened here?"

"I was trying to make some coffee for Herb, to sober him up," she replied. "He went crazy, Sherry. He started shouting and slapping me, and the coffee just went everywhere. I never cleaned it up. I forgot all about it when you came to take me to the hospital."

Sherry reached down and picked up the coffee can and set it on the table. She righted the chair. "Why don't you go ahead and get the things you need, Annette, and I'll take care of this," she said gently.

"You don't have to do that," Annette responded. "It's been here for a while, a few more days won't hurt. Besides, I've heard that coffee is good for floors," she said with a wry smile.

Sherry looked at her and chuckled. "Well, that may be," she said, "but it'll be a while until you can wield a dustpan and broom, my friend, so I'll be the kitchen maid for today." She located the broom and began sweeping the mounds of coffee together while Annette went into the bedroom and gathered her clothes and cosmetics.

11

Eric stopped by the deli and picked up some beer and potato salad. He was still puzzled by Annette's absence. He tried not to dwell on it, but it kept nagging at him. He really cared about her. They had gone out several times after the picnic, and each time he felt closer to her. She was a special woman. And he thought Annette cared for him, too, which made it all the more difficult to understand this sudden disappearance. It just didn't make sense. Herb didn't seem to know anything about it. *Why would he anyway,* Eric thought. She wasn't his love or concern, anymore.

Herb was preparing to put the steaks on the grill when Eric arrived. He had been thinking about what he had done to Annette. *I've got to be careful how I act and what I say tonight,* he thought to himself. *I don't want to give Eric the slightest indication that I know anything. He'd kill me for sure if he knew what happened. I'll have to watch how much I drink, which is not going to be easy, but I can do it if I have to.*

What puzzled him was where had she gone after he left? Did she go to the hospital? If so, why hadn't she gone back to her apartment? He was going to find out before Eric did. Eric had been making noises about filing a missing persons report, and Herb didn't need that.

"Hi, bro," Eric called through the screen door.

"Hi, come on in and make yourself at home," Herb said cheerfully.

"Thanks," Eric responded. "I brought some beer and potato salad from the deli."

"Great, just put them in the fridge."

"Want a beer now?" Eric inquired.

"Sure, why don't you open one for each of us," Herb said, as he turned to go out on the patio. Eric opened the beers and followed his brother outside. He sat down in one of the deck chairs.

"How are things going since Helen left?" he asked while handing a beer to Herb.

Herb cringed. He didn't want to talk about it. It was painful enough to admit that your wife had left you because of your drinking. He didn't want to dwell on it. "Oh, okay, I guess," he said absently. "I mean, I miss her and Casey, and all that," he said hastily, "but I'm getting used to them being gone." He took a deep swallow of beer.

"Do you talk to her often?" Eric inquired gently. He felt badly that his brother was going through this separation, but on the other hand, he didn't blame Helen for leaving. Herb had all but driven her out of the house with his drunkenness and temper.

"Oh, yeah, now and then," he responded. "She's at her mother's place. She seems happy." He paused. "I don't know, Eric. It's kind of a jumbled up mess."

Eric took a swallow of his beer. "I didn't come here to preach to you, Herb," he said, "but you brought it all on, yourself. You had said you were going to get help, then you didn't and kept on drinking. I don't think Helen really wanted to leave, but you were getting impossible to live with."

"I know, I know," Herb replied in a surly voice. "I'm going to get help. I just need some time." He felt a twinge of anger beginning to surface. He didn't want to lose control, not tonight. "Hey, let's talk about something else," he said. "Tell me about the meetings in Chicago."

Sherry and Annette were watching TV at Sherry's apartment. It was about 10 p.m. Annette had fallen asleep on the couch. Suddenly she awoke as a searing pain shot through her head. A cry escaped her lips and Sherry jumped at the sound. "What's the matter?" she cried, as she got to her feet.

"I don't know, exactly," Annette said. "All of a sudden I've got this horrendous pain in my head, and it's getting worse. Oh, Sherry, I can hardly see," she cried.

Sherry tried to comfort her. "I'm sure it's okay. Do you want to take a pain pill?"

"I took one just a little while ago. This is really hurting, Sherry. I can't stand it!" She struggled to get to her feet.

Sherry helped Annette to stand. She was concerned now. "Do you want to go to the hospital and have it checked?" she said.

"I don't really want to," Annette said, "but I think maybe I'd better. I haven't felt this kind of pain before, and it's throbbing like crazy."

"Okay, let me get my shoes on," Sherry said, bending down to look for them."

"I think mine are in the bedroom," Annette said, holding her head.

"Okay, I'll get them. You just sit down." Sherry flew to the bedroom and found Annette's sneakers, jacket, and purse. When she returned to the living room, Annette was leaning against the back of the couch, her face grimaced with pain. "Here, I've got your shoes," she said, as she knelt to help Annette put them on. "And I have your purse and jacket, too."

"Thanks," Annette said as she reached for them.

Sherry put on her own shoes, grabbed her purse, and turned off the TV. She helped Annette to her feet. Together they went down the steps to her car. Her heart was in her throat. She was really worried about Annette.

As they entered the hospital parking lot, Annette looked over at Sherry. "Déjà vu," she said, unsmiling. Sherry nodded. At the reception desk, Annette asked the woman if she could see Dr. Anderson, that she had been under his care earlier that week. He was off tonight, she was told, but a Dr. Weller was there. He was the other doctor who had seen Annette. She asked to see him.

The clock on the wall showed 11:30 p.m. There were a few people in the waiting room. A trauma case had just come in, someone who had been shot. A child screamed. His voice echoed through the hallway. Someone had been bitten by a dog, another had his leg in a makeshift splint. It was a typical Saturday night in the E.R. Sherry shifted in her chair. It seemed like yesterday when she was here with Annette the first time. She flipped mechanically through the pages of a dog-eared magazine. She wondered if Annette was all right. Or was she suffering a delayed reaction from the beating? *That creep*, she thought, *he should be held accountable for this.* She didn't know Herb, had never met him. She didn't really want to, either, except to give him a piece of her mind for doing this to

Annette. She hoped Annette would find some way to make him pay for her suffering. It just wasn't fair!

"Excuse me, Miss," a male voice interrupted her thoughts. "I'm Dr. Weller. Are you Sherry Adams?"

"Yes," said Sherry putting down the magazine. She glanced at the face of the man who sat down next to her. He looked concerned.

"Miss Adams," he began, "I just saw your friend, Annette Howard. She's going to have to be admitted to the hospital tonight. She's suffering severe head trauma from the injuries she sustained last week. We're going to put her in I.C.U. I'm sorry, I mean intensive care."

Sherry's mouth went dry. She knew what I.C.U. meant. Her heart began racing. "Oh, my God, what's happened to her? She was staying with me, and she was fine. She was asleep on the couch, and woke up, and had a terrible pain in her head, and . . ."

"It's all right, Miss Adams," Dr. Weller said gently, trying to comfort her. "Sometimes these things happen afterwards. We're going to take good care of her. Don't worry. Dr. Anderson will be here, and he will be in charge of her case. I'll be assisting him in surgery tomorrow morning," he said.

Sherry was close to tears. "Thank you, Dr. Weller," she said shakily. "I appreciate anything you're doing. I'll call tomorrow and see how she is. We're very close, almost like sisters."

"I understand," he said. "Thank you for bringing her tonight. She's in quite a lot of pain, and we're going to try and ease that as much as possible."

"Okay," Sherry said, as she stood up. "I'll leave my phone number at the desk, in case you want to get in touch with me." The doctor smiled at her and thanked her. She walked over to the desk, gave the receptionist her business card, and went out the door into the night.

Eric was doing some chores at his apartment. It was Sunday evening, and he was still thinking about Annette. *Maybe I'll try and call her again,* he thought. If she were out of town, she'd probably come back tonight to go to work on Monday. He dialed her number. It rang once, twice, three times, then a voice, her voice answered. "Hi, this is Annette . . ."

My God, it's her, he thought. "Annette, where have you . . ." he began.

". . . I can't come to the phone right now, but if you leave your name and number, I'll call you back as soon . . ."

His heart sank. It was her answering machine. But wait a minute, it hadn't been on before! All the times he had called, there had been no answer at all. So this meant she was back from wherever she had been. He decided to leave a message. "Annette, this is Eric. I've been worried sick about you. Please call me when you get in, any time, no matter how late. Please, I really want to talk to you." He hung up and stared at the phone, as if it could speak to him. *Please,* he prayed, *Let her be all right!*

Promptly at 7:30 a.m., Monday, Annette was wheeled into the operating room at Mile High Hospital. Surgery was performed on her by a team of doctors headed by Dr. Anderson and Dr. Weller. The procedure went well, and by early afternoon she was resting in intensive care.

Monday morning dawned hazy and warm. Eric scrambled out of bed at the sound of the alarm. He ran his hand through his hair and remembered—there had been no call from Annette last night. He felt dejected. *Was she playing games with him?* he wondered. He showered and dressed. He decided to stop by the diner and get breakfast, then he would call her at work. Surely she'd be there.

Shortly after 9 a.m. he called Smith & Wheeler and asked for her, only to be told she was out sick. *Again? Still? What was going on here?* he wondered. *Okay, then I'll talk to her friend Sherry. Maybe she knows what the sam heck is going on.* He asked to speak to Sherry, (hoping there was only one: fortunately there was) but he was told Sherry Adams was out of the office on an assignment and wouldn't be back until late afternoon. He left his name and number and said it was urgent.

Sherry had spent most of the day with an advertiser, trying to set up a promotional idea for her boss. She was doing more work in the field now, since her promotion. She was tired, and hadn't had much success. It was getting late, so she called the office and told a part-time employee that she wouldn't be back to the agency that afternoon. She was not told about the message from Eric, even though it was sitting on her desk. She decided to drive over to the hospital and see how Annette was.

The lady at the reception desk looked weary. "Can I help you?" she asked.

"Yes, I'd like to inquire about a patient named Annette Howard," she said. The woman scanned a sheet of paper attached to a clipboard. "Oh, she's in intensive care," she told Sherry. "No visitors allowed."

"I'd like to leave this card for her, when she's able to receive it," Sherry said, handing a light blue envelope to the woman.

The receptionist took the envelope and set it on her desk. "Certainly, I'll see that she gets it," she said, with a warm smile, which momentarily lifted the tired look from her face.

"Thanks a lot," Sherry said. She turned away and walked towards the outer doors of the lobby. She wondered how long Annette would be in intensive care. She was really concerned about her, more than ever.

Eric turned the page on his desk calendar. It was Tuesday. He hadn't received a call back from Sherry Adams. *Doesn't anyone return calls anymore?* he wondered. He dialed the number for Smith & Wheeler and asked to speak with her.

After a moment a pleasant voice greeted his ears. "Sherry Adams, may I help you?" He couldn't believe it, she was actually there!

He cleared his throat. "Yes, I hope so," he said somewhat hesitantly. "Um, this is Eric Woodward, and I'm a friend of Annette Howard..."

"Oh, yes," she said, interrupting him, "I'm sorry, I didn't get back to the office yesterday afternoon, and so I didn't get your message until this morning. I was going to call you later. What can I do for you, Eric?" She was completely taken off-guard by the message he had left. She hadn't expected he would try to contact her about Annette. He must really be concerned about her.

"Well, I thought maybe you could shed some light on what's happened to her," Eric said, a bit hesitantly. "I've been trying to get ahold of her, at her apartment, and also at work, for days. All they tell me is that she's out sick. There's been no answer at her apartment. Her apartment manager doesn't even know where she is, and," he took a breath, "since you seem to be a close friend of hers, well, I thought maybe you had heard from her, or know where she is. I'm really worried about her." He paused. "I know we only met once, and I'm sorry to impose on you, but..."

Sherry took a deep breath. "That's okay," she said, "It's no problem," She wondered what she could tell him. She couldn't tell him the whole story, but she had to tell him something. "Eric," she began, "Annette had a fall, and has been out of work for several days."

Eric listened intently. "A fall?" he repeated. "But where is she? Why isn't she at home? What happened?" he pleaded.

Sherry paused for a moment to collect her thoughts. *This could get complicated*, she thought to herself. "She's in the hospital," she finally said. "Look, it's kind of hard to talk on the phone right now," she said, trying to sound as diplomatic as she could. She didn't want to tell him any more.

Eric seized the opportunity. He felt deep inside him that she knew more about this. "Please, Sherry. I really need to talk to you about this," he said with concern. "Would you meet me somewhere, for coffee or maybe for lunch?"

Sherry swallowed hard. This was not going to be easy. "Well, okay, Eric," she said slowly. She just couldn't let him wonder about Annette. He was clearly disturbed about her. But she'd be careful what she told him, too. For Annette's sake, as well as hers.

"Do you have any plans for lunch today, Sherry?" he asked her.

"No," she said quietly, somewhat confused about what she was doing.

"Why don't we meet at Dino's on Larimer Street?" he said after a moment. "Do you know where that is?"

"Yes, I know where that is, Eric. That's fine. What time?"

"How about 11:30. We'll beat the rush."

"Okay, I'll meet you there."

"Thanks, Sherry, for meeting me. I really appreciate it," he said sincerely.

"You're welcome, Eric. I'm glad to help, if I can," she added, choking back a lump in her throat. God, this was going to be tricky. She hung up the phone. She halfway wished he had never called her. But on the other hand, someone had to tell him something, and it looked like it was going to be her.

Sherry was visibly nervous. *Why did I decide to meet him?* she wondered.

What could she tell him? Her palms were damp. I've got to stay calm, she thought. I'll tell him Annette had a fall in her apartment. That was true. The reason, however, would not be disclosed by her. She felt kind of sorry for this man. He really cared for Annette. He had sounded scared and confused. She wondered what he would do if he knew what his brother had done to Annette. She silently hoped she was doing the right thing.

A charcoal grey Honda swung into the restaurant parking lot and parked near the entrance. Sherry got up from the bench where she was sitting in the waiting area, and looked out the window of the door. A tall, dark-haired man in a pin-striped suit was coming up the steps. *That's him,* she thought to herself. She had only seen him once, but Eric Woodward was not that easy to forget. He was a very good-looking man. He opened the door. Sherry was standing in the alcove. He recognized her immediately and smiled. She took his extended hand as they greeted each other.

"Thanks so much for doing this," he said to her.

Sherry swallowed hard. "No problem," she said, with a casualness that belied her true feelings. "Like I said, I'm glad to help, if I can." She felt like a traitor. Eric inquired about their reservations, and they were seated in a quiet area of the restaurant. "Would you like a drink, Sherry?" he asked, as the waiter approached.

"Maybe a glass of wine," she said, "I'd like some White Zinfandel."

"Okay, he said and I'll have a glass of chablis. We'll wait a bit to order, if you don't mind." The waiter nodded and discreetly disappeared. Eric took a deep breath and looked directly at Sherry. "You said that Annette had been injured in a fall, and that she is in the hospital. How did it happen?"

Sherry gathered herself together. *Here goes,* she thought to herself. "I'm not really sure, Eric. It happened at her apartment. It was late at night. She called me and said that she'd fallen and hurt herself and asked if I would take her to the emergency room. I went over to get her and took her to the hospital. While I was there, the doctor said they wanted to keep her overnight for observation. Then they decided to keep her there for several days, because they thought she had a concussion, and she had quite a few other injuries."

"A concussion?" Eric exclaimed. "What did she fall on?"

"From what I understand, her head hit the edge of a table," Sherry said, glancing down at the napkin in her lap. She was getting a bit uncomfortable with all this. The waiter reappeared with their glasses of wine. He set them on the table and asked for their order. They looked at the menus, ordered chef salads, and the waiter left again. Eric took a sip of his wine.

"So all the time I was trying to call Annette from Chicago, she was in the hospital," he said solemnly. "No wonder I couldn't reach her."

"That's right," Sherry said, quietly. "And all they knew at work was that she had a fall and was out on sick leave. After she left the hospital, she came over to stay with me. The doctor didn't want her to be alone. She was taking medication, and he wanted someone to be with her." Sherry paused. *This was going okay after all*, she thought.

"So no one knew where she was, or what had happened to her, except you," Eric said. He looked at her with an intense gaze. His expressive brown eyes were almost penetrating her soul.

"That's right," she said, briefly glancing away.

"That explains the mail in her mailbox then, and why the apartment manager didn't know where she was," he said, slightly shaking his head.

"The apartment manager didn't know anything about it, and when Annette and I went over there on Saturday, the office was closed, Annette couldn't tell her anything. Also, Annette hadn't turned on her answering machine the night she got hurt, so there was no way for anyone to leave a message for her. We discovered that on Saturday when we went over to her apartment to get some things."

The salads arrived. The waiter placed a basket of bread sticks on the table. Conversation came to a halt. Eric asked if Sherry wanted another glass of wine.

"No thanks," she said. "I'd like coffee, please."

"Make it two coffees," Eric told the waiter. "Thanks." He began to eat his salad. "Poor Annette," Eric said, between mouthfuls. "I was so worried about her. I thought something had happened. And being hundreds of miles away, I thought the worst."

"She was really concerned about you, too, Eric," Sherry said, as she took a forkful of her salad. "She didn't know where you were staying in Chicago..."

"I know," he said. "I tried to call her and let her know, but I couldn't reach her at home. I left a message at Smith & Wheeler letting her know what hotel I was staying at, but of course, she didn't get that message, either." He paused. "What's her condition now, Sherry?"

Sherry took a swallow of wine. "While she was staying with me, she got worse, Eric. Saturday night I took her back to the hospital. They said she was having complications from the injury, and were going to perform surgery the next morning. They did, and she's in intensive care now."

Eric stopped eating. He laid his fork down on the table and stared at the woman across from him. A worried expression crossed his face. "Will she be all right?" he asked her.

Sherry noted the intense look of concern on his face. "They think she'll be okay, but it'll be a while until she recovers completely."

That was quite a be... a fall," she said quickly. She had almost slipped up and said the wrong word.

Eric closed his eyes for a moment. He shook his head. This was really upsetting. The woman he cared so much about, the one he loved, was suffering in the hospital from a stupid fall. He wished he had been here to help her, to be with her. "Which hospital is she in?" he asked Sherry.

"Mile High," Sherry responded.

"Oh, who's her doctor?" he suddenly asked. He knew several doctors at that hospital. After all, that's where he had been taken when he was recovering from the skiing accident.

"I'm not s-sure," Sherry stammered. She hadn't planned on his asking this. "But I'm sure she's getting good care."

"I know several doctors there," Eric said. "That's where I spent my recovery after I got hurt skiing. You know, when I first met Annette," he said, looking at Sherry. "I'm sure she told you about it."

Sherry nodded. Yes, she knew all about that. She felt like the walls were closing in around her. There was nothing she could do about the doctor situation. If Eric really wanted to know, he could find out who her doctor was, and maybe about how she got hurt. She didn't want any part of that. She stared at him. His lively brown eyes were moist. "I love her, Sherry," he said, his voice filled with emotion. "She the most wonderful woman I've ever met. I feel so badly that she's hurt." He looked her directly in the eye. "I'm so glad she has you as her best friend, and that you were there to take care of her when she needed it most."

Sherry was touched by his emotion. This guy is really sincere, she thought. He'd probably kill his brother if he ever found out that he was the one responsible for Annette's condition. "Thanks, Eric. That's nice of you to say. She is my best friend, and I think she's also very fortunate to have you to care about her." She smiled at him. She wished she could tell him what really happened, but it wasn't her place to do so. Maybe he'd find out someday, somehow. She hoped he would, so he'd know what a real jerk his brother was. How ironic. Annette was now in the same hospital he had been earlier this year. Wouldn't it be amazing if she had the same doctor? But the odds of that happening were pretty slim.

They finished their wine. Sherry picked up a bread stick and twirled it in her fingers. "Well, now you know why Annette wasn't around, and what happened to her," she said to the man sitting across from her. She hoped she had sounded convincing.

"I'm so grateful to you for letting me know about it, Sherry," he said honestly. "I was at my wit's end. It was a long shot to get ahold of you, but it was my last hope. I was about to go to the police and file a missing persons report. Nothing seemed to add up. No one knew anything, even Herb. It was weird. She had just plain disappeared."

At the mention of Herb's name, Sherry stiffened. *Why would Eric ask Herb about her?* she wondered. Maybe he was just asking everyone he knew. She wondered what Herb had told him. Whatever it was, it was a lie. She was pretty sure of that. "Now we both need to say a few prayers for her recovery," she said quietly.

12

The following evening, Eric arrived at Mile High Hospital. He walked into the lobby. It seemed strange to him to be there again. Only this time he wasn't the patient, he was the visitor and he had come to see how his dear Annette was. The lunch with Sherry had put his mind at ease, somewhat. Still, he was puzzled about how and why Annette had fallen. Sherry had seemed somewhat vague, and he was very concerned about Annette's condition.

He approached the reception desk. "I'd like to inquire about a patient here, named Annette Howard." The plump, middle-aged lady behind the desk glanced at him. She consulted a list on a clipboard. "Are you a family member?" she inquired.

"No, but I'm a very close friend. I've been out of town, and just found out that she had been hurt and brought here."

The woman looked closely at the tall, nice-looking man who stood before her. He held a single rose, wrapped in cellophane, and an envelope in his hand. "I'm sorry," she said, "but Miss Howard is in intensive care and cannot have visitors."

Eric sighed. He wondered if he should ask to see her doctor. Probably not. But then, why not? It couldn't hurt. "Um, excuse me," he asked her, "could you please tell me who her doctor is?" The woman hesitated. She wasn't supposed to give out that information to a visitor, but she felt sorry for him. He seemed so concerned, and he was a close friend. She'd tell him, she decided.

"Well, I probably shouldn't do this," she said very quietly, "because you aren't family, but there are two doctors, Dr. Anderson and Dr. Weller, handling her case. But don't tell anyone I told you, okay?"

"Sure, okay," Eric said to her. "Thanks so much." He couldn't believe his luck! He didn't recognize the name of Dr. Anderson, but Dr. Weller had been Eric's doctor when he had the skiing accident. "I know Dr. Weller," he told the woman. "He was one of my doctors when I was a patient here last winter. How can I reach him?"

The woman consulted a list on her desk. "He's up on the fourth floor right now," she said. Eric thanked the lady and headed towards the elevators. He rode to the fourth floor and got off. To his left he saw the nurse's station. He glanced at his watch. It was still visiting hours. He asked a pretty brunette nurse if he could see Dr. Weller.

"I'll have to call him for you," she said with a smile. "Who should I tell him is waiting?"

"My name is Eric Woodward," he said to her. "I'm a former patient of his. I was here after a skiing accident a few months ago."

"Oh, okay," she said, as she picked up the phone and dialed a number. She spoke into the receiver. "He'll be here in a few minutes," she said brightly as she replaced the instrument. "Would like to have a seat in the waiting area over there, Mr. Woodward?" She gestured towards a sitting area that had some chairs and a couch.

"Sure, that's fine," Eric said. "Thanks."

"You're welcome," the nurse said as she went back to work at her desk.

He sat down in one of the wooden chairs. He felt tired. He wondered if Dr. Weller would tell him anything about Annette's condition. He knew about the doctor-patient relationship. But he was also determined to find out how she was. A few minutes passed. Eric shifted in his chair. He waited a few minutes more, then he recognized the tall, angular form of Dr. Weller walking down the hallway towards him. He stood up and went to meet him.

"Hello, Dr. Weller," he said. "I'm Eric Woodward. I was a patient of yours several months ago."

The doctor studied his features. An instant look of recognition crossed his face. "Oh yes, Eric, I remember. The skiing accident. We were very concerned about you. How are you doing? It's nice to see you again," he said with a smile. "What can I do for you?"

"I'm doing fine, thanks. Actually I wanted to talk to you about a very dear friend of mine, Annette Howard. I've been out of town and found out that she had a serious fall and is here in intensive care. I understand that you and Dr. Anderson are handling her case."

"Yes, that's right," he said. Eric noted the serious expression that crossed his face. "Her head was badly injured, and she suffered complications as well. I think she'll be all right, but it will take some time. She underwent surgery yesterday morning."

Eric hesitated. "From what I was told," he began, "she fell in her apartment, and her head hit a table or something. A girlfriend of hers brought her to the hospital while I was away on a business trip."

Dr. Weller looked closely at Eric. He knew he had to be careful what he said. But he also wanted Eric to know there was more to Annette's condition than that. She had suffered a beating, and he was going to tell him. He didn't know who had done it, or why, but whoever it was was responsible for Annette's serious condition. He thought Eric should know.

"Well, that's partly true," Dr. Weller answered after a moment. "I think there's something you should know, Eric," Dr. Weller said as he took Eric's arm and led him over to the couch. They sat down. "She has injuries from a beating, as well. I don't know any details, but she suffered severe head trauma." He paused. "She's the woman who came to see you in the hospital, when you were injured in the skiing accident, isn't she?"

Eric glanced sharply at the doctor. "Yes, she and I have been seeing each other." He sat motionless. He was stunned. At the mention of the word "beating" his heart stood almost still. What was this all about? Sherry didn't mention anything about any beating. Who would have done something as terrible as that? An intruder? Someone she knew? His head was spinning with questions. "Are you sure about the beating?" he asked the doctor.

"Yes, Eric," he responded. Eric fixed his gaze on the eyes of the man who sat next to him. He couldn't believe this was happening. There had to be some mistake.

"Dr. Weller, Annette is the one who saved my life in the skiing accident. If it weren't for her, I wouldn't be here today. She went for help and got the ski patrol to rescue me from the valley. She's a wonderful woman, and I love her," he said, fighting back the tears that tore at his eyes. He looked down at the single, cellophane-wrapped, red rose that lay in his lap. "I had no idea someone beat her up," he said, with moist eyes. I was out of town and didn't know she had been hurt until yesterday. Oh my God," he said, as tears began to slide down his cheeks. He reached into his pocket for a handkerchief. He was completely overcome with emotion.

The doctor patted Eric on the shoulder. "I'm sure she'll be all right. But she'll need all the reassurance and caring you can give her, Eric, after she gets out of intensive care. I guess she doesn't have much family, only some relatives out of state. She seems like a real nice woman. It's a shame someone would do that to her."

Eric nodded. He was completely taken aback. "How long do you think she'll be in intensive care?"

"Well, the surgery went well. It depends on how she responds to the medication and treatment. I can't say for sure," Dr. Weller replied. "She's pretty sick, but I'd say about a week or maybe two."

Eric composed himself and took a deep breath. "Thanks, Dr. Weller, for letting me know about this," he said huskily. He handed the rose and card to the doctor. "Would you please see that she gets these?" he asked, glancing at his watch. "I've got to go now. I'll call in a day or so to see how she is."

"Certainly, Eric, I'll be glad to," he said. He stood up, as did Eric, and they shook hands. "I hope I haven't upset you too much about this," he said, "but I thought you should know, in case no one had told you."

"I appreciate it very much," Eric said. "I had no idea. I can't imagine who would have done that. I really care a lot for Annette, and I'll be praying for her."

"Great, I'm glad to hear it. Here's my card, Eric. Please feel free to call me if you like. I'll let you know how she's doing."

"Thanks, Dr. Weller. Goodnight." Eric turned and walked towards the elevators. He felt badly shaken. He hadn't expected anything like this. His dear Annette was in I.C.U. Suffering not only from a fall, but from a beating from some lousy creep. Who? Why? He was going to find out.

The week passed. Eric called every day to see how Annette was. Each day he brought a single red rose and a card to the hospital. Each time he was told her condition was the same. She was semiconscious, but appeared to be responding to treatment and medication—standard stuff. His calls to Dr. Weller brought almost the same response. He found it difficult to concentrate at work. The thought of Annette's beating haunted him. Several times he considered calling Sherry to ask her why she hadn't told him about it, but he didn't. Maybe she didn't know. Maybe Annette didn't tell her about it. Maybe, but they were such close friends. Besides, Sherry was the one who had taken Annette to the hospital that night. Surely she would have known. But why didn't she tell him? *Maybe she didn't want to upset him,* he thought. Or maybe Annette had asked her not to tell him. He had the unsettling feeling there was more to it than was being said.

Eight days later, Annette fully opened her eyes for the first time in days. She blinked at the light. A nurse stood at her bedside, smiling. "Hello," she said softly. "Welcome back to the real world."

Annette moved her head slightly. The pain was gone! The unbearable, excruciating, head-wrenching, throbbing pain was gone. She couldn't believe it. For days she had been in and out of consciousness, but each time the pain was there. And now it wasn't. She moved her arm. It felt somewhat stiff, but it moved without pain. The nurse left the room for a moment and then returned with a doctor.

"Well, look at you," Dr. Anderson said with a small smile. "How do you feel?"

"Like I've been asleep for a long time," Annette said, managing a smile. "But my head doesn't hurt anymore. It's wonderful."

"Good," he said as he took her pulse. "We've been very concerned about you. This is good news to see you awake and not in pain."

"How long have I been in here?" Annette inquired looking around the room. There was no dizziness, either.

"Oh, a couple of weeks," Dr. Anderson replied, "but I think we'll be able to take you out of I.C.U. and put you in a regular room now."

"That's great," Annette said. "You mean I can finally have visitors?"

"Yes, but don't overdo it. I don't want you to have a relapse."

"Okay," Annette said. She was somewhat tired, but happy. She could focus on people and things without her vision blurring. Without pain. Wonderful!

The door to her room opened. "I just heard about you, Annette," Dr. Weller said from the doorway. "How are you feeling?"

"I feel pretty good, Dr. Weller. My head doesn't hurt at all. In fact, I feel sort of hungry."

"Now that's a good sign," he said brightly. "We'll see about getting you something to eat, and later we'll get you moved out of I.C.U."

"Thanks, that would be great," Annette said, glancing at both doctors. "You guys are okay."

The two doctors looked at each other. "Well, that's nice to hear," Dr. Anderson said with a chuckle. He turned and walked towards the door, followed by Dr. Weller. "We'll see you later, Annette," Dr. Weller said, as he closed the door. He was smiling.

Sherry hung up the phone. She had just found out Annette was finally out of I.C.U., and was moving to her own room. It had been a long ordeal. She had prayed for her everyday, as well as called to see how she was. She would go and see her tonight, she decided. She wondered if she should call Eric and tell him the good news. Maybe I'd better wait until tomorrow, she thought. She wanted to see Annette alone, to tell her about her meeting with Eric. It would be a bit awkward if he were there, too.

A tall, youthful-looking brunette nurse opened the door to Annette's room. Her arms were laden with flowers and a large paper bag. In a vase were long-stemmed red roses. There was one for each day that Annette had been in I.C.U. The bag contained get-well cards, including those from Eric. He had brought one each day while Annette was in intensive care. The nurse smiled as she brought the bouquet over to Annette's bed.

"You've got to take a whiff of these," she said, holding the flowers close to Annette's face. "Aren't they wonderful?"

Annette reached out and selected one of the scarlet blooms. She held it close to her face, closed her eyes, and breathed in its sweet fragrance. "Oh, that smells so good," she said, touching its velvety smoothness. It was nice to be able to feel, touch, and smell again. She replaced the flower in the vase. "Who are they from?" she inquired.

"Well, I'd say you have quite an admirer," the nurse said, as she set the vase on a table. She handed Annette the stack of notes she had taken out of the bag. "Each one of the roses was brought separately, with a card," she said. Ever since you were brought to I.C.U. We've been saving them for you."

Annette slowly opened one of the envelopes. Inside was a beautiful get-well card signed, *With Love, Eric*. Emotion overcame her. She began trembling and a tear rolled down her cheek. The nurse quickly came over to her bedside. "Are you okay?" she inquired with an anxious look. "Should I get the doctor?"

"No, I'm all right," Annette answered. "I'm just a little overcome by all this," she said, gesturing towards the flowers and the envelopes that were sprawled out on her bed. "He must have been here every night. Oh my goodness, this is incredible," she cried.

"I'd say that he really cares a lot for you," the nurse said, smiling at Annette. "You're really fortunate to have a guy like that."

Annette continued to open the envelopes that lay before her. Inside each one was a lovely get-well or thinking-of-you card, signed *With Love,* or *To Annette, the Love of My Life.* All them were from Eric. She had been in I.C.U. for a little over two weeks and there was a card for each day. She began to cry. She couldn't help it.

The nurse appeared with a box of tissues. She, herself, was close to tears. She had never seen anything like this in all her six years of service at Mile High Hospital. This must be quite a guy, she decided. She watched as Annette wiped her eyes and felt happy for her. She had been through quite an ordeal.

Along with the cards Eric had brought, there were others from Sherry and co-workers at Smith & Wheeler. Her sister and other friends and relatives had sent cards, after they learned Annette's disappearance was caused by a hospital stay. However, among them was one card Annette wished she had never opened, never received. It was from Herb. He mailed it to the hospital. It was very simple. Its only message scrawled inside was *I'm Sorry!*

Dusk was falling as Sherry reached the hospital parking lot and found a place within a reasonable distance from the entrance. She gathered the floral arrangement into her arms and walked towards the lobby. Inside, she checked at the desk for the location of Annette's room, and took the elevator to the third floor.

Annette was sitting up in bed when the door opened. At the sight of her friend, she grinned and held out her arms. "Hi, stranger," she said with a smile.

Sherry set the flowers on the table, next to the vase of roses, and quickly crossed the room to the bed. She gave Annette a big hug. "Hi, yourself," she said. She felt her eyes misting. She released Annette and smiled down at her. "How're you doing?"

"I'm doing okay, Sherry," Annette answered. "It's really good to see you again. They weren't sure what to do about me. I guess I was fading in and out for a while, but the doctor said I'm doing good. It'll be a few days, however, until I can go home."

"Well that's to be expected. After all, you went through a hell of a lot," Sherry said. She pulled a chair over next to the bed and sat down. "It's really great to see you, and I'm glad you're doing so well. I miss you so much at work. Oh, I brought you some flowers,"

Sherry said, glancing over at the table. I see someone sent you roses. They're beautiful."

Annette looked over at the flower arrangement Sherry had brought. "Thanks so much for the bouquet. That's really sweet of you." She then stared at the stately red blossoms in the green glass vase. "The roses are from Eric, Sherry. He was here every night since I was in I.C.U. Every night he brought a rose and a card. The cards are over there, too, It's unreal!"

"He must really love you a lot, Annette," Sherry said quietly. She was wondering how she should tell her about the meeting with Eric. "Listen, there's something I have to tell you," she said with concern. "I don't want you to get upset, but you've got to know."

"What are you talking about?" Annette asked warily.

"Well, it all started when I got a call at the office from Eric," Sherry began, "and he was frantic, wondering if I knew where you were and if anything had happened to you." Sherry proceeded to tell Annette about her meeting Eric for lunch, and that she had simply told him Annette had suffered a fall and was in the hospital, recovering from surgery.

"You didn't say anything about Herb, or what he did to me, did you?" Annette asked, a worried expression on her face.

Sherry was quick to put Annette's fears to rest. "No, absolutely not," she said, shaking her head. "I told him you had fallen at your apartment, hit your head on a table, and that you stayed with me after you were released from the hospital. I told him you got worse, and had to go back to the hospital, had surgery and was in I.C.U. That's all. Annette, I couldn't tell him about Herb. It wasn't my place to do that. And I knew you didn't want him to know. But I had to tell him something, and what I said was true. It just wasn't the whole story. I hope you don't mind my doing that. He was really concerned about you, and was ready to go to the police and report you missing!"

"What? You're kidding," Annette said.

"Nope, I'm serious. Annette, that guy really loves you."

Annette leaned back against the pillows. She reached for the glass of water on the hightstand and took a swallow. She shut her eyes for a moment. "I guess you're right, Sherry," she said suddenly, opening her eyes. "I love him, too. I've been kind of afraid to say it, or to show it very much. The chemistry has always been there, but I didn't trust my feelings and I didn't want to be hurt again. There's no doubt in my mind now. He is so caring and considerate, much more so than Herb ever was."

"He's pretty easy to look at, too," Sherry said with a grin. "He has the most incredible eyes."

Annette smiled. "Yeah, he sure does," she agreed. "I'm glad you met with him, Sherry. Thanks. He doesn't need to know all of what happened. Maybe someday I'll tell him about it. I doubt if Herb ever will."

"Yeah, I doubt that too," Sherry said with a shrug. "It's too bad Herb has such a drinking problem. It's probably ruined his life in many ways."

Annette looked thoughtful. "I feel sorry for him, despite what he did to me," she said. "He's really not a bad person, Sherry. He's sort of insecure, and has got to come to grips with alcohol and what it does to him. He just can't handle it. Helen left him. I guess I would've left too, if I were married to him." She paused. "He did send me a card. Inside it he just wrote *I'm Sorry*."

Big deal, Sherry thought to herself. He should be sorry enough to help pay for some of her medical bills. But that wasn't her business. She patted Annette's arm. "Well, he's not your problem now, so don't worry about it. Everyone at work sends their best, and hopes you'll be back soon. I guess you got some cards from the group there."

"Yes, I did, even a really nice one from Hal. Please tell them all thanks from me, and for the flowers they sent, too."

"I will," Sherry said. "Well, I guess I'd better go." She glanced at her watch. "It's getting close to the end of visiting hours." She rose from the chair and gave Annette a hug. "Get some rest, and I'll see you soon," she said.

"Okay. Thanks for coming. I really have missed you, too. This is one of the most boring places in the world, trust me. I can hardly wait to get out of here."

"We'll make up for lost time, after you're well," Sherry said, smiling.

"Sounds good," Annette said happily. She waved to her friend as she went out the door. "Bye!"

Sherry waved back. "Bye, see you later."

Annette sighed, and closed her eyes, and laid her head back on the pillows. She felt tired, but content. The room was quiet. She didn't hear the door open. There was a soft click as it closed. Probably one of the nurses, Annette thought vaguely to herself. She was aware of a presence in the room, but nobody moved or spoke. Strange. An almost overpowering feeling came over her. Her eyes flew open. She couldn't believe what she saw. Before her stood a tall, dark-haired man holding a single red rose, wrapped in cellophane. It was a mirage. It had to be. Annette blinked hard. No, there was no doubt. He was real. He was here. Her breath caught in her throat. She felt tears tugging at her eyes.

He crossed the room in long strides. She felt his strong arms enfold her. He held her for a long moment, then gently kissed her hair. "Annette. Oh, Annette, I've missed you so much," he whispered huskily into her ear. He moved his cheek close to hers. She felt the dampness of his face, smelled the aroma of his cologne. Her fingers touched the sweet roughness of his jacket. "God, I've been so worried about you. I thought I'd lost you," he said as he choked back tears.

Annette shook her head. The tears fell freely now. She didn't try to stop them. She reached for a tissue. "I think I need one, too," Eric said as he looked at her. His eyes were brimming. "I love you, Annette," he said, his voice shaking.

Eric sat on the edge of her bed. He remembered the rose and handed it to her. Annette took it with trembling fingers. "Thank you," she said softly, "and for all the others, too." She gestured towards the vase with all the roses he had sent. He nodded. "They're beautiful," she said. "I didn't realize you had been here every day."

"I wasn't allowed to see you, but I wanted you to know I was here, and that I cared," he said in an emotion-filled voice. He kissed her lightly. The nurses and doctors said they would see that you got them. Looks like they did.

Annette stared at him. She felt so much love for this man. "This is quite a turnabout isn't it," she said, with a small grin. "The last time we were together in a hospital, you were in the bed and I was the visitor."

Eric grew serious. He took her hand. "Annette," he began, not sure exactly how to approach the subject, "I know what happened to you, and I'm so sorry. I wish I had been there to help you." He looked intently into her eyes.

"Oh, it was just one of those things," Annette said, totally unaware of what he meant. "I fell and hurt my head, and things got pretty complicated. I understand Sherry met with you and told you about it."

Eric was puzzled. "Yes, she told me about that. I was frantic, Annette. I didn't know where you were, or what had happened to you. I kept calling, but there was no answer. Your apartment manager didn't know where you were, but your car was there. I called your office, but all they told me was that you were out sick. It's like you just disappeared off the face of the earth." He paused for a moment. "So I decided, as a last resort, that I would try and contact your friend Sherry, at work. I figured you two were close friends, and that maybe, just maybe, she had an idea of where you were."

"She was my saving grace, Eric," Annette said solemnly. "If it hadn't been for her, I don't know what I would have done." She looked away. "I didn't know how to get in touch with you. And I discovered, afterwards, that I had forgotten to turn on my answering machine that night, before I went to the hospital."

"It must have been a nightmare for you." I wish I had been here to help," Eric said. He gently touched her cheek. "Who did this to you, Annette? Why would someone want to hurt you like this?"

Annette stiffened. "What do you mean?" she said warily. She was suddenly frightened.

Eric hesitated. Maybe he shouldn't bring it up until a later time, he thought. But he was anxious to find out what had happened, and who was involved in this act of violence. "Annette, I've been told you were the victim of a beating. I want to know who did this horrible thing to you. Did someone try and break into your apartment that night? What happened? I really want to know."

Annette couldn't believe what she was hearing. How did he know? Who would've told him? It wasn't Sherry. She was sure of that. But who? Not Herb, she thought with certainty. What do I do now? she wondered to herself. Maybe it was one of the nurses? Oh, God, I didn't want this to happen. I didn't want him to know, she thought to herself. "Who told you that?" she asked him. Her throat felt dry.

Eric looked down for a moment. "It doesn't matter who told me, Annette, that's not important. What is of concern is who's responsible." He waited.

She looked at him with puzzlement. "No, no one broke in or anything like that," she said finally. "Eric, it isn't important. It's all over and I'm doing fine. What have you been up to lately?" she asked him, trying to change the subject.

But Eric would have none of that. "What do you mean it isn't important?" he said, gazing sternly at her. "You've just gone through surgery, and spent weeks in the hospital because of injuries you suffered from someone beating you." He raised his voice. "How can you possibly say it isn't important? Whoever is responsible should be locked up. No one has to endure that kind of abuse."

Annette turned her head away. "Don't make a big deal of this, Eric," she pleaded. "It's over. I just want to forget about it okay?"

"Did you know the person?" Eric inquired.

Annette hesitated.

"I said, did you know the person, or was it a stranger?" Eric pressed.

Annette began to tremble. Tears started cascading down her face. "I knew him," she said, her voice barely a whisper. She put her hands over her face. She hadn't wanted things to be like this, and she was still afraid to tell him.

Eric felt badly that he had upset her. "I'm sorry, Annette," he said gently. He took her into his arms. "I just think that whoever did this to you should be held accountable, and possibly put away so they can't do it to someone else."

"I'm sure he didn't mean to hurt me," Annette said after a moment. "We were having a discussion, and things just kind of got out of control." She didn't want to tell him it was Herb, his drunk brother, her former lover. She just couldn't bring herself to do that. It would create problems neither one of them needed. "It's okay, Eric. I appreciate your concern, but I think it's better to leave it alone."

"Okay," Eric said without conviction. "If that's the way you want it." He was really confused and concerned. It was obvious she was trying to protect someone. But why? Who? One of her former boyfriends? A co-worker? He was going to do everything he could to find out. "It's quite ironic," he said with a bit of a smile, "that one of your doctors is Dr. Weller. He was one of mine when I was here after the skiing accident. He's the one to whom I gave most of your roses and cards."

"You were here every night," Annette said, with wonder in her voice.

"Yes, I was," Eric said gently. He looked deeply into her eyes. "I love you, Annette. I really love you, and I was so worried about you."

Annette smiled. "I love you too, Eric," she said. "It took me a while to realize it, but I really do." He took her into his arms again and held her. He wanted to make everything right for her. She was his special woman, and he was going to see to it that she was well cared for. Forever.

"The main thing now is for you to get well," he said finally. "If I don't leave pretty soon, they'll throw me out. I think visiting hours have been over for a while. We're lucky they haven't discovered I'm still here."

"No problem," Annette said, with a wry smile. "I'll just get them to bring in another bed for you."

Eric grinned. "What do you mean another bed?" he said, laughing. "There's plenty of room in this one!"

"Yeah, sure," Annette said. She laughed too. She looked hard at him. This was the man she loved, no question. She could hardly wait to get out of here to explore that probability. He loved her, too. She felt safe, content. Things were going to be all right after all. But little did she realize that soon both their lives would become caught up in a whirlwind of turmoil.

13

Annette was discharged from the hospital a few days later. She spent a couple of days at home, and then was able to return to work. She and Eric were together constantly. He hadn't mentioned anything further about what had happened to her. He still wondered about it. She had tried to put it all behind her. Things seemed to be going well for them until one evening, when a phone call set events in motion that would change the pattern of their lives forever.

They were at Eric's apartment on a Friday evening. He was fixing dinner when the phone rang. He answered. It was a fairly lengthy call, and when he hung up, he looked faintly worried. "That was Herb," he said to Annette. "It looks like we'll have to go to New York for a few days. There's a firm that's interested in a computer program we've both worked on, and Herb's boss wants us to present it to the company. I think I mentioned this to you earlier, only the trip was postponed from the original time."

Annette remembered. He had told her about it over dinner at the Italian restaurant, their first date. She had felt a strange feeling come over her then. She felt that way now. "When do you have to leave?" she asked him.

"On Monday," he answered.

"That doesn't give you much time to get everything ready," she said.

Eric looked concerned. "No, it doesn't. I wish Herb had told me sooner. He knew about it before now. He's been drinking a lot again. It really worries me, Annette."

Annette moved away. She made a pretense of setting the plates and silverware on the dining table. She couldn't seem to shake the uncomfortable feeling that had settled over her.

"I'll probably have to work all day tomorrow, and possibly on Sunday for a while, too," Eric said with a sigh.

Annette went over to him and put her arms around him. "I'll be glad to come and keep you company," she said, smiling up at him.

He looked down at her. He ran his finger gently down her cheek. "You know how much work I'd get done if you did that," he said and chuckled. "Not that I'd mind, but somehow I think it'll have to be Herb and the computer keeping me company."

Annette removed her arms from around him. "Well, okay," she said with a note of resignation in her voice. "Let's eat, I'm hungry." She tried to sound light and cheerful, but she didn't feel that way.

"Sounds good to me," he said as he put the food on their plates and carried them to the table.

"What time do you leave Monday?" Annette asked him.

"I think we're booked on a 7:00 a.m. flight, but I'm not sure. I'll let you know."

She hesitated. "How long do you think you'll be gone?"

"Probably a couple of weeks. I'll call you and let you know where we're staying. I guess the secretary of Herb's boss is making all the arrangements. Damn it, I wish he'd given me more notice. I've really got to get a lot done before we go," Eric said with disdain. He sounded upset and concerned. He glanced over at Annette. She was toying with her food. "I thought you said you were hungry."

"I was, I mean I am," she stammered, laying down her fork.

"What's wrong, Annette?" he asked gently.

"Nothing, really. I don't know," she said absently. "I just wish you weren't going away again."

Eric's eyes narrowed. "Are you afraid that the person who hurt you will try and do it again?" he asked, suddenly frightened at the thought.

"Oh, heavens, no," she said quickly. "There's no danger of that, I'm sure." And of that she was really sure. Herb would be gone too.

"What then?" Eric asked, as he pushed his chair back and came around to her side of the table. Annette stood up and they embraced.

"I guess it's that I'll just miss you terribly," she said finally, trying to put her fears to rest. It wasn't the real reason, but she didn't dare voice how she felt deep inside. She didn't trust Herb. She didn't exactly know why, but the feeling was strong.

"Oh, sweetheart, I'll miss you too." Eric said as he held her close. He kissed the top of her head. "It's only for a couple of weeks or so. When I get back we'll go out for a special dinner somewhere, okay?"

"Sure, okay, that sounds great," she said, smiling at him. "I'm sorry, I know this trip is important to you and your job. I hope things go well."

"I hope so too, Annette. This could be a big breakthrough for our company, if the firm in New York likes the computer program we've done. It could be quite lucrative for both companies. We'll have to wait and see." Eric sat back down at the table and began to eat. Annette swallowed over the lump in her throat. She took a sip of ice water. Her stomach was churning. She didn't feel like eating now.

"Has Herb been doing a lot of work on this program?" she asked him.

"Yeah, when he's been sober," Eric replied sarcastically. "He's really a smart guy and has great ideas, but he's been drinking so much lately that he's been hard to work with. Maybe this trip to New York will help. At least I'll be there to try and keep him sober and thinking straight."

Annette thought to herself, It'll probably take more than you and a business trip to New York to do that. She had no way of knowing, nor could she or Eric have dreamed in their wildest thoughts, that what was about to happen, hundreds of miles away, would impact their lives for a long time.

The weekend went quickly. Eric spent all day Saturday, and Sunday afternoon at his office. He and Herb worked on the final details for the presentation of their computer program. Sunday evening Eric stopped by to see Annette. She was watching TV when he rang the doorbell.

"Hi," she said warmly, as she opened the door.

"Hi, sweetheart," he responded, as he came through the doorway and embraced her. They kissed briefly, Eric sat down wearily on the couch. Annette turned off the TV and sat down next to him.

"How's it going?" she inquired. "Did you get everything done that you had to hoped to do?"

"Well, we did as much as we could. I think we've got a pretty good presentation. We'll see what happens in New York. I'm a bit nervous about it, but I'm sure things will go all right."

Annette looked at him. He looked tired. "I'm sure it will all go fine," she said, trying to sound optimistic. "Do you want a cup of coffee, or maybe a beer?"

"No, thanks. Coffee would keep me up all night, and beer right now would probably put me to sleep on my feet." He smiled at her, and squeezed her hand. "I'd better get going and finish packing. I just wanted to come by and see you. We leave at 7:00 a.m. tomorrow morning."

Annette leaned against him and put her head on his shoulder. "I'm glad you came by. I'll miss you."

"I'll miss you too, honey, a lot. I'll call and let you know where we're staying."

"Okay," she said, not wanting to move, but knowing she should.

Eric stood up and pulled her into his arms. "You're the most wonderful thing that has ever happened to me," he said, looking deeply into her eyes. "I love you so much." He kissed her soundly. "That will have to last until I get back," he said, then added, "please be careful, Annette. I don't want to come back and find you in the hospital or something."

Annette smiled. "Don't worry, I'll be fine." She kissed him and walked him to the door. "I love you, Eric," she said. "I'll be praying that things go well in New York."

"Thanks, hon, I'll see you soon," he said, as he hugged her. "Goodnight, Annette."

Annette sat down on the couch. Her thoughts about Eric's trip to New York were somewhat clouded. She couldn't shake the feeling of uneasiness she felt. It had shadowed her for the past few days. At least I don't have to worry about Herb coming here drunk again, she thought to herself. And I know if Herb gets out of hand, Eric can handle him. But she couldn't quit worrying. Everything is going to be fine, she tried to tell herself. But some of her unknown worst fears were about to become a reality!

The next morning, Herb and Eric took the 7 a.m. flight to New York. It was an uneventful trip. They landed at JFK airport and took a taxi to their hotel. They were to meet with the principal executives of Trans Financial Corporation early the next day. They arrived at their hotel and began unpacking.

"Do you want to get a sandwich or something to eat?" Eric asked.

"Yeah, let's go down to the coffee shop and get something," Herb replied.

"Okay," Eric said, as he finished unpacking his suitcase. "Why don't we take the charts down with us, and go over them while we eat. I want to be sure we've covered everything."

Herb didn't want to do that. He was tired of working, of his life, of everything. He really hadn't wanted to come on this trip, but he was told to do so. And his brother had to come. Eric had worked on this program, too. Herb didn't want to acknowledge that. He wanted the credit. After all, it had been his idea. But Eric had put the program together. "Oh, let's leave it alone for a while," Herb said in a surly voice. "We'll have plenty of time to work on it later."

"Well, all right," Eric agreed, somewhat reluctantly. He was anxious to check on the details, and be sure their figures were right.

"Let's go to the lounge first," Herb said. "I'm thirsty." Eric didn't think it was a good idea. He was afraid Herb would start drinking, a lot. He didn't want that to happen, especially now. He looked at his brother.

Herb was reading his mind. "Don't worry, bro," he said, grinning. "I'm not going to overdo it. I just want a drink before we dine."

Eric relaxed a bit. "Okay," he said. "Maybe that's a good idea after all. Let's go find the lounge."

That night, Eric called Annette and told her they were staying at the Royal Plaza Hotel. She wished him good luck on their presentation. He told her he loved her and would see her in a week or so. He hung up the phone. Herb was looking at him. He had a strange look on his face. "You really are nuts about her, aren't you?" he said.

Eric stood up and walked over to the window. He felt somewhat uncomfortable. "Yes, Herb, I am," he said, looking at the lights of the city that sparkled in the distance. "I've never felt this way about any woman before. She's wonderful."

Herb sat on the edge of the bed. He looked down at the floor. "Yeah, she's quite a woman," he said gruffly. "Who would've ever thought you'd fall in love with my ex-lover. Unbelievable!"

Eric turned from the window. He glanced at his brother. There was a smirk on Herb's face. Eric couldn't quite read the meaning. Was Herb jealous? Was he unhappy about Eric's relationship with Annette? He didn't know. Herb had never said anything about how he felt, and Eric had never asked. He assumed their relationship was all in the past. He had no clue how much rage and jealousy had built up inside his brother. He had no idea that soon it would be uncontrollably unleashed on him!

The next morning, promptly at 9:00 a.m., Eric and Herb walked into the eleventh floor conference room of the corporate offices of

Trans Financial Corporation. They met with the executives of the firm, and both men gave their presentation of the computer program. The meeting lasted into the lunch hour, and a catered lunch buffet was served. That afternoon the meeting continued, and by the end of the day, both Eric and Herb were exhausted. The acceptance of the first section of their program was a positive beginning. They both looked forward to giving the balance of the presentation the next day. After that, they would be showing the employees of the firm how to input and access the Concord Engineering program in their computers. If everything went smoothly, Eric figured, they would be able to leave New York on Friday evening, or Saturday morning at the latest.

14

Eric and Herb were having a drink in the Green Patio Bar. It was their last night in New York. Their business meeting had ended, and everything had gone well with the acceptance of their computer program. The people at TFC were pleased and very grateful to the two men from Concord Engineering.

"Well, I'm glad that's all over," Herb said. He took a big swallow of his drink, and motioned to the waiter for another.

Eric nodded. "I'm glad it's over, too. It went better than I thought it would."

"Why, didn't you think they'd accept it?" Herb said loudly.

"Oh, sure, but you know how these big corporations are. You have to paint them a picture, and they have to be sure that the program will work for them."

"Yeah, it sure will work out well for them," Herb said, "and we'll get the big bucks."

The waiter brought his drink. He drained the glass before him, and took the fresh one from the tray. Eric watched him. He was going to have to be careful not to let Herb drink too much.

"My boss will sure be pleased with what happened," Herb said. "I might even get a promotion." He took another deep swallow of his drink. He had almost finished it.

Eric took a swallow of his. "I think Concord should give both of us a promotion. That was a lot of hard work, Herb. You really had some great ideas, and I helped you put them together."

"Yeah, guess that's right," Herb said, as he motioned to the waiter for another round.

"Hey, let's cool it on the drinks, Herb," Eric said with some irritation in his voice.

"What's your problem?" Herb said to him. "I want another drink. What? Our work is over. It's time to celebrate."

"Celebrate, yes, but not get drunk," Eric said. It was the wrong thing to say.

"Whadda you mean?" Herb stammered. "I'm not drunk." He raised his voice. "How dare you say I'm drunk."

"I didn't say you were drunk, Herb," Eric said quietly. "I just said we shouldn't get drunk." He didn't want Herb to drink any more, but he was hesitant to say too much about it. He knew Herb's temper only too well.

"You do whatever the hell you want. I want another drink," Herb shouted. "Waiter, com'ere," he commanded. He waved his arm wildly in the air. "You know what the matter is with you?" he shouted at Eric. "You don't know how to have any fun. You never do anything wrong. You're the purrfect brother. You always were the one who got everything."

Eric was getting concerned now. Herb was beginning to get loud and out of control. It could happen quickly. He had seen it before. "C'mon, Herb let's go have dinner," Eric said, trying to wean his brother away from the alcohol. It didn't work.

"I don't want dinner yet," Herb said, glaring at Eric. "I wanna another drink."

Eric tried to use psychology. "Look, I'm starving, Herb. We can come back here later and have another drink. You'll feel better after you eat something. It's been a long time since we had lunch."

Herb was irritated by Eric's words. "I want to drink now," he said, pounding his fist on the small wooden table. Eric glanced around. There were a lot of people in the bar and it was noisy, so no one had noticed, yet. But that wouldn't last long, he thought. Herb was getting louder and more demonstrative.

"You think you're so great, Mr. High and Mighty," Herb shouted. "Well, you aren't as great as you think. All my life I've wanted things that you had." He took another swallow of his drink. "Then, I had something you didn't. Annette." He glared at his brother. "But you, you S.O.B., you got her anyhow. I wanted her. I loved her. But you got her, damn you! I hate you for that!"

Eric was taken aback. Herb was really getting out of control now. He had to get him out of here soon, without creating a scene. But that wasn't going to be easy. "Look, Herb," he said trying to calm him down, "that's all over with. You and Annette broke up. You went back to Helen. That was your choice."

Herb wasn't listening. And he didn't want to hear what Eric was saying. He finished his drink in one big gulp. He looked at Eric and his eyes narrowed. "That's none of your damn business," he growled. "I wanted Annette. I still want Annette." An evil gleam came into his eyes. "I almost had her that night, too," he said, glowering at his brother.

Eric stared at him. A glimmer of recognition passed across his face. His mind churned. He was suddenly afraid of the meaning of Herb's words. He put his hand firmly on Herb's arm. "What are you saying, Herb? What do you mean you almost had her that night?"

Herb pushed Eric's arm away. "That's right," he shouted. "I almost had her, only she fought like an animal, the little bitch." The rage and jealousy that had festered for years inside him was finally being released. He didn't care what he said or did. He hated his brother for loving Annette, for having what he didn't have, for being what he wasn't, and never would be.

Eric felt the blood leave his face. He was stunned. It was clear to him now. Herb was the one, the one who had beaten Annette. She hadn't wanted Eric to know. Eric had never considered Herb. It never entered his mind that he was capable of doing such harm. He was enraged! He stood up and grabbed Herb by his collar.

"You bastard," he screamed. "You're the one. You're the one who beat her up that night at her apartment, aren't you? Answer me, you lousy creep."

The patrons in the bar were looking at them. Eric threw some money on the table. He started pushing Herb towards the doorway. "Get out of here before I kill you," he shouted.

They both stumbled out the door. On the sidewalk Herb pushed Eric away and started laughing. It was a deep, hollow laugh. "Yeah, I'm the one, little per-fect brother," he yelled to Eric. "She didn't tell you, did she? She wanted to make love to me. I know she did, but she was sooooo committed to you. Yeah, I still love her. And I know she loves meee, even though she fought me off that night." He paused for a minute. "But it's her own damn fault she got hurt. She asked for it."

Eric pulled Herb around and smashed his fist into his face. He had had enough. He was so angry and hurt, Blam! He hit him again!

Herb recoiled and tried to hit Eric, but he was too drunk. His swing went wild. Eric grabbed Herb by the lapels of his jacket. He pushed him against the wall of the building.

"How could you do that to someone?" he roared. "Especially someone you cared about? Don't you realize how badly she was hurt? You no good, drunken lousy creep." Eric was besides himself. He hit his brother again. He wanted to kill him for what he had done to Annette. "You're no brother of mine," he shouted. "I don't care what happens to you."

A small crowd had gathered. They watched the altercation between the two men. Herb's face was bleeding. He was waiting for an opportunity to break away and he saw his chance when Eric let down his guard for an instant. He pushed Eric away from him, then ran out into the street to where their rental car was parked. He had the keys in his coat pocket. In a flash he was in the car and had started it. Eric realized what he was doing and ran over to the car. He started pulling on the passenger side door, and pounding on the fender, shouting for him to stop. Herb ignored his attempts, put the car in gear, and hit the accelerator.

Eric watched, dazed, as the tail lights of the car disappeared down the street. He was shaken. He couldn't believe what had just happened. He had never hated his brother, until now. At this moment, he despised him more than he ever thought he could.

Herb drove erratically down the street. He wanted to go somewhere and drink, and just forget everything and everyone. He passed several bars. He sort of knew the area as he had been there several years ago. There was a tavern he vaguely remembered called the Plaid Peacock. He couldn't recall the street name, but he had an idea where it was, if it still existed. In his quest, he turned down several side streets before finally seeing the blue and red neon sign in the shape of a peacock. There, that was the place! He pulled into the rear parking lot and, after some creative moves, parked the blue Ford rental car. He looked in the rearview mirror. His cheek was beginning to swell and his lip was cut where Eric had hit him. The bleeding had stopped, but he looked sort of roughed up. He decided to go in the back entrance and into the men's room to clean up a bit before he entered the bar.

Eric leaned somewhat unsteadily against a bench on the sidewalk outside the Green Patio bar. The hotel was about a mile away. He could walk to it or take a taxi. He decided to walk to clear his head, to think. The realization that his brother was the person who had beaten Annette was overwhelming. He couldn't believe it! The man was crazy! He was insanely jealous of him and of his relationship with Annette. Now what? Herb had been drinking a lot and had taken off with the car.

Eric's hand hurt and he was getting a bad headache. He had no idea where Herb had gone, but it was probably to another bar to drink. Eric didn't want to run into him, not now. He was still very upset. He had lost it when Herb had told him what he had done to Annette. He walked a few blocks. There was a bench nearby and he sat down, suddenly overcome with emotion. He bent over, his head in his hands. He felt the tears starting, and let them fall unchecked.

Herb washed his face and combed his hair. He glanced in the mirror and straightened his tie and smoothed his shirt. Not too bad, he thought. He left the men's room and went into the bar. It was crowded and dark. Good, he thought to himself. There were no tables available, only a seat at the bar itself. He sat down and ordered a drink. The bartender glanced at him. He thought he looked like he'd been in some kind of fight, but he seemed to be okay and didn't appear to be unduly under the influence. Herb could mask the effects of alcohol so well. He had mastered it over the years. He took a big swallow. The cool spiciness tasted so good!

Eric sat on the bench for several minutes, then he composed himself and got up. He started walking in what he thought was the direction of the hotel. He wondered about calling Annette. No, he thought. I'm too upset to call her right now. I'll wait until I see her in person to tell her what happened. He wondered what her reaction would be when she knew her secret was no more, and how he had found out.

It was after midnight when Eric got back to the hotel. He went up to the room to find Herb wasn't there. He wasn't really surprised. He wondered if he was in the hotel lounge. Maybe he should check and see. He left the room and took the elevator to the lobby floor. There he got off and walked into the Camelot Lounge. It was crowded. He looked around, but didn't see Herb. He took a seat at a table and ordered a beer. He was exhausted and felt terrible. He had no idea Herb was so jealous of him and of his relationship with Annette. Nothing had ever been said. But Herb was like a coiled spring that had just come unwound. Eric wondered how he could ever take back the things that had been said. They both had lost control. It had driven a big wedge between them, and now they were supposed to work together.

Herb finished his third drink. He was feeling no pain. One more and he would leave. He really didn't want to go back to the hotel. Eric would be there and he didn't want to face him. He never should have told him about that night, but he was so angry with his brother for loving Annette and for having her love him back. She was someone he had once cared about, and still did. Eric hadn't had any idea it was he who had beaten Annette.

Herb took another swallow. Damn it! Why was he always the one who lost out? Even Ted, his other brother, had been successful. Herb began thinking about how Ted had been killed in an auto accident. Only Ted hadn't been drinking, the other driver had. Herb drained the contents of his glass. He set it on the counter and got up from the barstool. He threw some money on the bar and walked unsteadily to the front door of the tavern.

Outside he looked around for the car. Nothing looked familiar. Then he remembered he had gone in the back door. He walked around to the parking lot in the rear of the tavern and wandered through the sea of parked cars. But he was unable to find the rental car. After a while he got disgusted. "Oh the hell with it," he muttered "I'll just forget the car and take the subway back to the hotel."

He knew there was a subway line at the 47th Street station, which was nearby. He briefly thought about taking a taxi back, but decided it would be too long a wait. He began walking to the station. The wind brought a chill and he wished he had brought his overcoat. The streets were almost deserted. He reached the subway entrance and used the railing to steady himself as he went down the trash-laden steps. He put the token in the turnstile and went through to the platform area.

There was no one around. It was eerily quiet. Herb wandered over to the side of the platform closest to the tracks. He stood looking down the darkened tunnel. He glanced down briefly at his watch. One fifty-five a.m. As he looked up, he suddenly lost his balance. He reached out for something to grab on to, but it was a futile attempt. There was nothing there. He felt himself falling. A throaty scream escaped from his lips. He hit something hard, something cold. Excruciating pain, then darkness enveloped him.

Eric awoke from a deep sleep. A blaze of sunlight streamed through the window. His head pounded. He had a strange feeling something was wrong, but his head was so groggy he didn't know what was going on. He glanced at the bed next to his. It hadn't been slept in. Herb hadn't come back to the hotel at all last night. He dimly wondered if he passed out in some bar somewhere. He slowly got up, went over to the TV, and turned it on. It was about ten minutes to eight.

He went into the bathroom and splashed cold water on his face. It felt good. A cup of coffee and a couple of aspirin would make him feel a lot better. He took a quick shower and grabbed his electric razor. As he shaved, he wondered how he was going to find Herb. They were supposed to fly back to Denver later today. Eric wanted to call the airline and reserve space for them on an afternoon flight. Suddenly his thoughts were interrupted by a voice coming from the TV set.

"... Manhattan Police have reported that a man apparently fell from the 47th Street Station Subway platform late last night, and was believed to have been hit by an oncoming train. He has been identified as Herbert Edwards, 32, of Denver, Colorado. Edwards was pronounced dead at the scene. Police are continuing their investigation. A taxi driver was robbed of $200 last night..."

Eric was completely stunned. He sank down on the edge of the bed. The razor dropped from his hand to the floor. He didn't notice. "Oh my God," he cried. "No, it's not true, it can't be. It must be a mistake. This has got to be a nightmare," he shouted. "Oh my God..."

He shut his eyes as if he could make it to be a dream, but it was all too real. He had seen and heard. He had to get himself together. He'd have to call the police station. He would have to take care of things. He rose from the bed and, like a robot, finished shaving and got dressed. He felt numb. He saw Herb's suitcase on the floor. Tears dimmed his eyes and streamed down his face. He pounded his fist on the bathroom door. A flood of guilt swept over him. Herb had confessed to beating Annette. They had fought. Eric had hit him, said things to him that now he could never take back or apologize for. He hadn't really wanted anything to happen to Herb, he was just angry with him, and upset. But Herb would never know that now. He had died thinking his brother hated him. Eric reached for the phone book to call the police.

The taxi driver left Eric off in front of the police station near where the accident had occurred. He stood for a minute looking at the drab grey building looming in front of him. He took a deep breath, walked up the stairs, and opened the door. Before him he saw an information desk. Behind it, a uniformed officer was sipping a mug of coffee and reading a newspaper.

"Excuse me," he said to the officer. "I, uh, don't know who I should speak with..."

The man looked up. "What's it about?" he inquired.

Erica tried to keep his composure. "My name is Eric Woodward, and I heard, uh, on the news this morning that my brother Herb Edwards was killed in an accident in the 47th Street Subway station last night." He paused for breath. He was about to lose control.

"Oh, okay, just a minute," the officer said. "I'll get someone to help you." He picked up the phone and dialed a number.

"Thank you." Eric cleared his throat. He was trying to remain calm, but it wasn't easy. People were milling about. Voices seemed to be floating in the air. He didn't feel that any of this was real. It was like watching a movie, but somehow he was the main character. A few minutes later another officer appeared, and spoke to Eric.

"Are you the one who's here about your brother being killed in the subway?" he asked.

Eric swallowed hard. "Yes. I'm not sure what to do or where to go."

"Okay, here's what you have to do. Your brother's body was taken by the medical examiner. You'll have to contact that office to see about identifying him. I'll get the address for you." He went over to the desk and took a card out of his pocket and wrote an address on it. He gave it to Eric. Eric thanked him and left the building. He looked at the address on the card. He had no idea how far it was from the police station, so he hailed a taxi.

About fifteen minutes later, Eric found himself walking up the steps of the building that housed the medical examiner. As Eric entered the building, he was met by the examiner, who led him into a room that, at first glance, appeared to be full of oversized safety deposit boxes in a bank vault. Then the examiner opened a door and slid out the tray. Slowly he pulled back the sheet that covered the body to reveal the death-pale face of Herb. The examiner told Eric Herb had died instantly, and that his blood alcohol level was extremely high. He then asked Eric to confirm the identity of his brother. Eric felt a wave of nausea come over him. It was the hardest thing he had ever had to do in his life.

15

The phone rang in Annette's apartment. It was Saturday morning and she had planned to sleep late. She had worked overtime and was tired. But the voice on the other end of the line brought her instantly awake.

"Annette, this is Eric." It didn't sound like him. There was something strange about his voice. He sounded like he was close to tears.

"Eric, what's the matter?" she asked.

"Annette, I don't know how to . . ." He paused. ". . .How to say this . . ." He began sobbing.

"Eric, what is it?" she cried. "Where are you?"

"I'm in New York, Annette. Herb has been killed in an accident."

"What?" she felt a chill go through her. She caught her breath. "Oh my God, Eric no. How did it happen?"

"He . . . he fell from a subway platform, and . . . and was hit by a train."

Annette sat motionless. She was stunned. She couldn't believe what she was hearing. "Oh, Eric, I'm so sorry," she said. She felt herself close to tears.

"He'd had a lot to drink, Annette. We had been out together, last night, after the meeting was over. He got drunk and confessed he was the one who beat you up. I got furious with him. I lost control and hit him and said some awful things. He was so angry and jealous. About me. About you and I. I never realized that before. Then he got mad and took the car and disappeared. I never saw him again." Eric paused. "I don't know why he was at the subway station. Maybe the rental car ran out of gas. I don't know. I don't even know where it is. I feel so awful, Annette. I feel responsible. If we hadn't fought.... If I hadn't said all those things to him ... if ..." he choked back a sob.

Annette listened. She was trembling. What a terrible thing to happen to Herb. And poor Eric. "Eric, it isn't your fault," she said, trying to comfort him. "Herb had a problem. He couldn't handle alcohol, and he always blamed everyone else for his actions."

"I know, but ... I'll never see him again ... to tell him that, in spite of everything, I did care about him. I didn't really hate him. But he'll never know that."

Annette wished she were there with Eric, to put her arms around him, to comfort him. She, too, felt somewhat guilty. If she had told Eric before, that Herb was the one who had beaten her, maybe they wouldn't have fought. Maybe things would have been all right. "When are you coming back?" she inquired.

"I don't know for sure. I had to go and identify his body this morning, and I'll have to make arrangements to have it sent back to Denver. I'll also have to go to TFC on Monday and let them know what happened. I don't know what they'll want to do with the program now, depends on how things go. I guess sometime Monday night or Tuesday morning. I'll call and let you know."

"I wish I were there with you right now," Annette said, her voice shaking.

"I wish you were too, sweetheart," Eric replied. "I really miss you, and need you."

"I'll be praying for you, Eric. Please try not to blame yourself for all this."

"Yeah, I'll try," he said huskily. "I'd better go now. I'll talk to you soon. Good-bye, Annette. I love you."

"Good-bye, Eric. I love you too. Take care of yourself. Things will be all right." She slowly replaced the receiver and began to cry. "Oh, why did this happen," she sobbed into her pillow. "Why?"

Eric had called Annette from a pay phone in the lobby of the medical examiner's building. He felt completely drained. He took a taxi back to the hotel. There was a message for him from the rental car company. He checked with the desk and extended his stay for a few days so he could get things taken care of. He went up to the room and called the rental car agency. He was told that the car had been found by the police in the parking lot of the Plaid Peacock. It was undamaged, and had plenty of gas. They asked Eric if he wanted to continue to use the car. He declined. He was puzzled why Herb had left it there and taken the subway. Maybe he was so drunk he couldn't drive. But why hadn't he taken a taxi? Whatever the reason, Eric would never know, and that upset him a lot. He fell across the bed. He was totally exhausted and slept until the long shadows of night fell.

On Monday morning, Eric arrived at the Trans Financial Corporation offices. He was met by one of the vice presidents, and ushered into the president's office.

"Mr. Woodward, I can't tell you how sorry I am to hear about your brother's death. I heard about it on the news, and I was shocked."

"Thank you, Mr. Anderson," he replied. "I'm also in a state of shock right now. I was wondering what you want to do about the computer program we presented to your firm."

"Well, we'll have to have a meeting with the Board members, and the computer division. We'll let you know what their decision is. I hope we can work something out."

"I hope we can, too," Eric said. "I'm sure Concord Engineering will make the program available for your employees to use right now. However, the future is unclear at this point." He finished his meeting with the officers and thanked them. As he was leaving, many of the employees stopped him in the hallway and wished him condolences on Herb's untimely death. They seemed to be almost as shocked as he was.

He left the building and started walking up Madison Avenue. The throngs of people passing him on all sides seemed to be moving at a breakneck pace. With the exception of the call to Annette, he hadn't been able to grieve. He had to be in control, to take care of everything that needed to be done. He had made arrangements for Herb's body to be flown back to Denver on the same plane he was booked on, tonight. He had to call Annette and let her know what time he would be arriving. And he had to call his parents and tell them what had happened to their other son. That would be the most difficult thing of all. He hadn't been able to bring himself to do that yet, but he knew he had to. He walked for a while, then went over into a nearby park. Some young boys were chasing each other around the lake. He watched them for a few minutes and thought about his brother, and all the things they had done together. He began to weep.

16

Annette got to the airport early. Eric's flight would be arriving in about an hour. She gazed out the window at the mechanical birds moving slowly on the tarmac. Their blue and red lights traced patterns of color in the darkness. He had told her he was bringing Herb home on the same flight. His parents would be there, too. Annette felt numb. She still couldn't believe it. The man she had once loved, and then hated. The one who had hurt her physically, but who still believed he loved her. And she, him. He was dead. It was almost too much to bear. Now she had to be strong for Eric. He felt so guilty. She felt a gentle touch on her arm. She turned and was face to face with his mother. She embraced her. The tears were shining in her eyes. "I'm so sorry, Mrs. Woodward," Annette said to the woman, as tears began falling down her own face.

"Thank you, Annette," she said, between sobs. "I know you and Herb had your differences, but he really cared for you."

Annette choked on her tears. She hadn't expected this. She didn't know what to say now. She wondered if Helen would show up at the airport, too. She hoped not.

The announcement of the flight from New York came over the P.A. system. Annette and the Woodwards went over to the area where the passengers would deplane. Annette's heart was in her throat. She was trembling. She could see the lights of the aircraft as it approached the gate, then the jetway was pushed out to meet the plane. The passengers began walking down the walkway to the terminal. A large crush of them came into the waiting area, but not Eric. The three of them waited patiently, then they saw him. He looked tired, and sad. He saw them. He set down his briefcase and coat and put his arms tightly around his parents. They hugged for a long moment. Then he went to Annette and embraced her. She could feel the tears sliding down her face. He looked into her eyes. She could see the pain and grief mirrored in his eyes. He kissed her and held her close.

A few minutes later an airline official approached and asked for Eric. He was in charge of arrangements for the casket that had accompanied Eric on the flight. Eric excused himself and went with the man to sign the paperwork, then he made sure everything was in order for getting Herb's body to the funeral home. He didn't want his parents to have to worry about the details. Afterwards he joined Annette and his parents upstairs in the airline lounge. "Well, everything's taken care of," he said, as he sank into one of the plush blue seats. His father nodded at him.

"I'll call the funeral home tomorrow and set up a time for the viewing and the services," Eric said, glancing at his mother. She looked exhausted. "Why don't you both go on home. There's nothing more to do here. I'll be over in the morning and we can decide on what kind of service and all of that."

"I called Helen and told her what happened," his mother said suddenly. "She was really upset. I think she was seriously thinking about going back to him. I feel so badly for her and Casey."

Annette took a deep breath. She hadn't thought much about how all of this would affect Helen, until now. She had a son to raise, his son. She felt very uncomfortable.

Eric looked at Annette. He saw the discomfort on her face. "I'll call Helen and talk with her, Mom," he said. "I'll make it as easy on her as I can, even though Herb was drunk when it happened. He had an extremely high level of alcohol in his blood, and I don't think he even knew what hit him. He didn't suffer. I'm sure of that."

His mother cringed. She rose from her chair. "I think we'll go, Eric. It's getting late."

Eric embraced her, then turned to his father. "Get some rest. I'll call you in the morning." He hugged him hard.

"Goodnight, Eric," they said to their son. "And goodnight, Annette. Thank you for coming."

Annette put her arms around the older couple. "Goodnight, take care of yourselves," she said.

Eric watched them walk away. "It really hit them hard," he said. "First they lose Ted, now Herb. They never could accept the fact that he was a drunk. They loved him, even though it was a different kind of love than it was for Ted and me."

Annette put her arm around Eric's waist. She didn't know what to say. She had wanted to comfort them, but she didn't know how. There was too much in the past—she and Herb. Now, she and Eric. She didn't know how they really felt about her. Time would tell, she thought.

"Shall we go?" he said as he turned towards her. "I'm exhausted."

"Yes, let's do. Eric, come stay with me tonight. I want to be close to you."

"You have no idea how much I want to be close to you, too, Annette. This isn't over yet, I need you. I need your strength and love and caring, more than you know."

"I'm here for you, Eric. No matter what. I love you, and I always will," she said as she gave him a big hug.

By the time Eric and Annette reached her apartment, it was midnight. Annette unlocked the door and they went in. Eric sat wearily down on the couch, while Annette went into the kitchen. "Would you like a drink?" she asked him.

"I think I would," he responded. "What do you have?"

"Vodka, bourbon, and some rum, I think."

"How about a bourbon and water."

"Sure," she said, as she took the ice cube tray out of the freezer. She fixed his drink, and poured some vodka and tonic into a glass for herself. She carried the drinks into the living room. Eric's head was leaning back against the top of the couch. He looked exhausted. She handed him the glass.

"Thanks," he said, and took a deep swallow of bourbon. Annette sat down next to him and took a sip of her drink. She set the glass down.

"This has been a very long day for you," she said.

He nodded. "Yeah, it's been one of the longest and most depressing that I can remember," he said. "I just can't forget the sight of seeing Herb lying on that cold, metal tray. He was so pale, so still, so . . ."

"It's okay, Eric. I know you're devastated by this. I'm pretty shook about it myself." She moved closer to him, and put her arms around him. He began to cry.

"I'm sorry, Annette," he sobbed. "I'm having a hard time with this."

"It's all right, Eric," she said, trying to comfort him. He put his arms around her and they held each other close. She felt her own tears sliding down her face.

A few minutes later, Annette moved slightly away from him. "Let's go into the bedroom," she said to him. "I want to be close to you tonight."

He looked intently into her eyes, and then kissed her. "I want to be close to you, too, Annette."

She got up from the couch and took his hand. He followed her into the other room. She undressed and slipped between the cool, fresh sheets. He got into the bed, and they reached for each other. He felt her silken flesh next to him. He kissed her passionately and felt her body respond. "Oh, Annette, I love you so much," he whispered in her ear.

Annette returned his kiss. "I love you too, Eric," she said breathlessly. Their bodies entwined. Their tide of passion grew. The crescendo reached its climax. They found pleasure and comfort in their expression of love, and lay spent in each other's arms.

A couple of hours later Annette awoke. She lay in the dark for a while, listening to Eric's even breathing. She felt troubled. She could only guess how deeply Eric felt the loss of his brother, but she knew it was a lot. She tried to go back to sleep, but it eluded her. Finally she got out of bed, put on her robe and went into the living room. A glance at the clock on the VCR showed it was 2:37 a.m. She sat down on the couch and put her head in her hands.

She felt partly responsible for Herb's death. The guilt was almost overwhelming. Tears filled her eyes. If only I had told Eric it was Herb who hit me, she thought. Maybe none of this would have happened. Maybe Herb and Eric wouldn't have fought. Maybe he wouldn't have gotten so drunk and wandered off to the subway station. He'd still be alive. . . . She stifled a sob. Her thoughts were interrupted by a shuffling sound.

"What's going on?" Eric said sleepily as he came into the room.

Annette hesitated. "Nothing," she said. "I just couldn't sleep, that's all." She wiped the tears away with her fingers.

Eric came over to her. "What's the matter, Annette? I woke up and you weren't there and I was concerned. You sound like you've been crying."

"Oh, Eric," Annette suddenly cried, "I feel so awful about what happened. I feel partly responsible for Herb's death. If . . . If only I had told you about what had happened that night in my apartment, that it was Herb who hit me, maybe you two wouldn't have fought, and he wouldn't have gotten drunk and gone off by himself and tried to kill himself in the subway station. Maybe he'd still be alive." She burst into tears.

"Whoa, wait a minute," Eric said, as he sat down next to her. "The police said it was an accident. He had been drinking so much that he apparently lost his balance and fell. I don't think he jumped off the platform on purpose."

"But, maybe he wouldn't have drunk so much, and you wouldn't have fought about what happened that night, and . . ."

Eric put his arms around Annette. "Look, I feel responsible, too. I lost control. I don't know, it was such a shock to hear what he had done to you. And he was so, so sarcastic about it, and taunting me. I got really upset and angry, and said some things I'll probably always regret. Herb was very jealous and insecure, and he was angry with me." He paused for a moment. "It was a number of things, Annette, not just about him hurting you that night. Something probably would have happened to him sooner or later. Somehow he would have destroyed himself. If not with alcohol, then it would have been something else. He was a very unhappy person."

Annette trembled in his arms. "I'm sorry I didn't tell you it was Herb who beat me up, Eric. But I was afraid. I thought if you knew who did it, you'd try to do something to him. I wasn't really trying to protect Herb, I just didn't want anything bad to happen. I thought I was doing the right thing, but it didn't turn out that way," she sobbed.

"And Sherry, did she know what happened?" he asked quietly.

Annette hesitated. "Yes. She knew. Eric, I told her not to tell you. She wanted me to tell you about it, but I just couldn't bring myself to do that. I'm so sorry."

Eric held her close. "It's all right, Annette," he said, gently caressing her hair. "We both have to learn to forgive ourselves. And, I'm sure, we will in time. It might be kind of rough for a while, but we'll make it, together." He paused. "Look, I know this isn't the most romantic proposal, with candlelight and wine, but, I love you Annette, and I want you to be my wife. I want to be with you forever."

Annette looked at him with misty eyes. "I can't think of anyone

I'd rather spend the rest of my life with, Eric. I love you so much." They kissed and held each other close.

"There'll be a lot of things to take care of concerning Herb," he said after a few minutes. "But we could probably have a spring wedding, if you'd like."

"That would be nice," Annette said. "Maybe we could have it outdoors."

"In the rain," Eric said, with a small smile.

"There's that beautiful garden at the church," Annette said. "It would be perfect for a wedding. I'd like to be married there."

"We'll see what we can work out. And we'll go look at rings next week." He looked at Annette. "I know I've said it before, but you're quite a woman, Annette."

She smiled at him. "And you're the love of my life, Eric Woodward."

The day of the funeral dawned with leaden skies. The service was simple and appropriate. Many of Herb's co-workers came to pay their last respects to a man whose intelligence they admired, but who they never really knew. Most had no idea he lived in his own private hell. He had hidden his alcohol problems so well. A chilly, intermittent rain fell on the procession as it made its way slowly to the graveside. Eric and Annette stood solemnly as the casket was unloaded from the hearse and the pallbearers took their places on each side. Those attending the outdoor service shivered in the cold, blustery, late October wind. Annette noticed a woman, dressed in black, with a black veiled hat in the front row of the mourners. She held on tightly to a small boy's hand. She knew instantly it was Helen and Casey. Annette's heart gave a leap. She would finally meet the woman who had changed her life. Herb's life! She wasn't sure she was ready for this, but she had no choice. After the service was over, Eric took her arm and guided her towards where the woman was standing.

"Annette, I'd like you to meet Helen, Herb's wife," he said quietly.

The two women stood looking at each other. Annette held out her hand. She looked at Helen's tear-streaked face. She felt her insides shaking. "I'm glad to meet you, Helen," she said with more confidence than she really felt. "I'm so sorry about what happened to your husband. He was a good person." She hesitated slightly. "I-I was a friend of his."

A frown of recognition creased Helen's forehead. "Thank you,

Annette. That's very kind of you. I know that H-Herb t-thought a lot of you," she stammered, looking down at her son. "This is Casey."

Annette swallowed hard. Her gaze fell on the child standing there before her. This was the moment of truth. If there had ever been a doubt, there was no longer. He was a miniature version of Herb! She didn't know what more to say. She had finally met Helen and Casey, the woman and child who had shadowed her life. The chapter had ended. Eric embraced his sister-in-law. "If you need anything, just give me a call," he said with sincerity.

"Thanks, Eric, I will," she said with a quiet sob. She turned away. Casey let go of her hand. He went over to one of the floral arrangements that stood nearby. He grabbed a pink rose in his childish hand, then bent down and put it on the ground next to his father's casket.

"Is da da gone?" he asked his mother. She gasped and choked back tears.

"Yes, Casey, he's with God up in heaven, now," she said, wiping her eyes.

Annette and Eric both became teary-eyed at this exchange. They looked at each other for a long moment, then started to walk away. Annette turned and briefly looked back. The sight of the grieving widow kneeling with her son was too much to bear. They had both experienced love and pain with this same man. She hoped Helen would find happiness again someday. She felt no ill feelings toward her, only sadness. The past was over. A new future lay ahead for her and Eric. Time would heal the guilt they both felt. They would help each other through this. She took his arm and together they walked down the hill to the car.